Published in 2021 by FeedARead.com Publishing

Second edition

British Library C.I.P. A CIP catalogue record for this title is available from the British Library.

For Chris

Cast

Surgeon Robert Gentlepaw - friend of
Toby Hunter - superb cat detective
Prince Hector - heir to the throne
Princess Alexandrina - his fiancée

At the Red Windmill

La Chanteuse - singer
Dicky Bowpaws - compere
Victoria Gingersnap - dancer
Miss Redclaw - manager
Mittens - her maid Bradley
'Bells' Bellringer and
Richard 'Buttons' Greywhisker - a comic duo
Tinker - a Ribbon dancer

At the Grand Hotel

Corin Fluffs - hotel proprietor
Miss Cache - hotel head of staff
Benson - receptionist
Miss Grimclaws - head housekeeper

At the Races

Earl Greyfur - aristocat
Timothy Bobbins - jockey

Also featuring

Lillia Pinkpaw - schoolkit
Gertie and Vera Fluffs - adventuresses
Miss Silvia Startail - actress
Lucinda Lexington - actress
Fairpaw - an artist
Blackie - landlord of the Black Horse

1

DECKCHAIRS

I stretched out my back, paws and toes as far apart as I could reach, and chuckled to feel the heat baking the fine fur on my stomach. A deep red filled my eyes as the sun washed through my eyelids, and a salty breeze, with a hint of mackerel, tickled my nose.

"This is the life, Hunter - we should come here every year!" I declared to my companion, the detective Toby Hunter, who was sat bolt upright beside me. He looked far less comfortable, digging his claws into the sagging sailcloth of his blue striped deckchair as if it might give way at any moment.

"You know, they are very comfortable if you give them a chance." I added, rolling on my side to observe him more fully.

"Disgusting modern inventions," snipped Toby. "Hardly dignified, is it, to lounge like that in public?"

I was about to protest, when the curl of his lower lip betrayed a joke beneath his icy demeanour

"Besides," he added, "How can I observe my surroundings properly from such a low angle?"

I sat up and surveyed the scene. The beach was covered with bodies; male and female cats, kits to mollies, some in bare fur, some with a modest bonnet or sunshade, some more cautious older kits cloaked in white 'sunbathing' robes.

"Holidaymakers!" I declared. "No detection required here. It's a bank holiday, and the world and his wife has come to Brighton!"

"Hmph" Toby sniffed. " I think you forget, Robert, that we at least are not here on holiday." I sighed and acquiesced.

"You must agree though, it is rather hard not to be in a holiday mood on a beach in such weather."

"Well, at least this beach has the merit of being very short on sand; the blasted stuff is impossible to shift from the fur. When we got back from Alexandria I was brushing it out of my coat for weeks."

Our last adventure had led us to Egypt, and the heat of England's south coast was a pale echo of the intense blast from the African sun. Still it served very well for the end of May.

"Stop being so grumpy" I remonstrated. "Where are we going for lunch?"

Toby rolled his eyes. "I have given it very little thought, being more preoccupied with the problem we have been summoned to address."

"You don't know what it is yet!"

"Correction, Robbie, I do not yet know the precise nature of the problem, but I know, or can surmise, something of the nature of our client. And that suggests several interesting possibilities."

"Well, Prince ..."

"Ssh," he hissed, "Not here!"

"Oh Bast's Whiskers! What have you been staring at then?"

Toby waved an expressive paw at the scene before us. "What do you see? Ah yes, you have already told me - happy holidaymakers. An uncomplicated idyll. But that, Robert, is because you project onto the view before you the emotions sloshing about in that amiable brain of yours. You are happy and so everyone you see must be in the same cheerful state. Look more closely. Observe. That couple three down and to our left. Are they content?"

I looked cautiously. A cat may stare, it is only natural, but it is inviting a swipe to the nose to stare too hard at a gentlecat and his molly in a state of relaxation on the beach. The couple seemed ordinary enough. He had sleek brown fur, she was a disarming pure white. A discarded bowler hat on the pebbles beside them suggested the male owner was here for the weekend, ordinarily a London cat. He had a slightly tense expression, drawn about the mouth and eyes. His companion looked more relaxed, a pink ribbon about her neck giving sharp relief to her piercing blue eyes. These, I was horrified to note, were staring right back at me. I averted my gaze and delivered my findings.

"They've come away from London for the weekend. She's happy enough, he looks a bit peaky. Probably hungry."

Toby smiled. "Well that's a start. That gentlecat I should guess is indeed here from London. I rather doubt that his companion came with him. She, I suspect, is a local mollie, and has offered to show this cat the town - at a price."

"How do you know she's local?" I objected.

"The ribbons. Haven't you noticed them? A good third of the young female cats on this beach have them about their necks. Clearly a local fashion - I've seen nothing quite like it in London. In fact they seem to come in quite a limited range of colours. Either pinks, blues, yellows or black. Very few black though - pink is the colour of choice - this season at any rate! Still I have deduced something else from your own observations."

"What's that?" "Unless you are fed a premature lunch very soon, I shall get no more sense out of you this morning. Come, I hear the seafood on the promenade is sublime."

We abandoned our chairs, leaving a generous tip for the beach manager, and strolled up to the undercliff. A row of pale green arches in the high wall separated the upper coast road from the lower promenade. It was a pleasing broad walk, lined with gently waving palm trees, and sheltered from the coastal winds. Cheap food and trinket stalls, vending prawns grilled to order, iced creams, wooden buckets for kittens, and salted cream candies, littered the path to the left. To the right a series of more expensive bars and restaurants filled the archways, promising a mix of local specialities, almost exclusively fished from the sea. We entered a promising looking fish bar, under a pale yellow archway that had been recently repainted. A nervous looking owner placed us in a prominent table by the window, looking out to sea. An initial survey revealed it was thinly populated, but our presence seemed to encourage passers-by and a steady stream of promenaders filed into the restaurant as we ate. By the time dessert arrived, the restaurant was almost full, and our patron seemed greatly cheered.

"A fine meal." I said, licking my lips. "And this looks good!" Dessert was a flavoured iced cream, tinged with mint and black salt.

But a glance at Toby, pushing away his offering after a cursory lick, reminded me of our primary mission.

"Out with it, then" I sighed.

"Prince Hector has summoned us here, in his own words, 'to assist a friend with a matter of delicacy'. What does that suggest to you?" asked Toby.

"Well I suppose, for a start is it for a friend, or for himself?"

"Precisely. I suggest the latter."

"What makes you say so?"

"Almost any friend of the Prince must be in a less delicate position than himself - so far as the risk of public embarrassment must go. So why would not the 'friend' approach us himself, rather than embroil so illustrious a person?"

I nodded at this reasoning. Prince Hector is of course well known to the nation. Our King in waiting, he has notoriously mis-spent his youth, holiday-making both on the continent, and at his seaside palace in Brighton, humorously dubbed by his court as 'The Sandcastle'. But the anxious hopes of the nation had received a boost just this Spring, on the announcement of the Prince's engagement to Her Royal Highness, the Princess Alexandrina of Gothany.

"So you think it is...a female at the heart of this matter?"

"Undoubtedly. And to embroil the future King of England, she must be a very formidable person indeed."

"And quite unprincipled!" I declared, hotly "But surely - if that is the nature of the matter, it is - hardly worth your trouble, saving the Prince's noble person?"

"I am surprised that he thinks it a matter for a detective, though I can well imagine he is loath to involve the police. If it is a mere intermediary to blackmail he seeks, then I can think of better ones. Still - who can argue with a fat cheque from a Prince?" Toby reclaimed his dessert and scooped up a large spoonful, with a smile.

2
THE SANDCASTLE

The Sandcastle was set at a jaunty angle to the coast, some few hundred yards back from the sea. It was a curious and unique construction, festooned with fat bulbous domes, looking for all the world as if some giant had dribbled them onto the building with wet white sand. The style was some horrible and unnatural blend of Indian and Chinese, though it was a mercifully bland cream in colour, in contrast with the riot of golds, reds, yellows and blues within. Rumour had it that the fashionable architect who had designed it had based it quite closely on some Yooman predecessor building, on a nearby site, whose ruins were now lost to time. Crueller rumour had it that the domes resembled nothing so closely as the ravaged figure of the Prince himself, fatly dissipated by a diet of cream, indolence and vice. The building was set in extravagant gardens, though happily nature has as yet no means of rivalling cat's worst constructions. Tall vibrant plants in reds, blues and yellows thronged beside the paths, and exotic palms, kept precariously alive in one of the balmiest climates

England can offer, oversaw the paintbox. A few gardeners toiled watering and weeding as Toby and I took the meandering path towards the front gate. The gardens themselves were open to the public, in an initiative no doubt designed to endear the Prince to the local population. I hope they may have enjoyed the opportunity to survey his palace up close whilst assaulted by a thousand alien scents and sights, some compensation for the enforced confiscation of the land on which it was built. A small queue of visitors was ahead of us, a melange of tradescats and aristocatcy. These were ably and rapidly sorted by the butlercat, who was flanked by two soldiers, bristling with ironmongery. Tradescats were ushered towards a side entrance, presumably into the staff quarters, invisible from the front. Friends of the Prince were waved ahead with a bow. Inappropriate hopefuls and nobodies were firmly turned away. Still he seemed puzzled at our appearance, until Toby produced the passnote, enclosed with the Prince's letter. The butlercat took it from him, with a careful glance at the seal, and examined our faces more closely. Toby's face he might well have recognised, had he read the newspapers in recent months. Toby's recent triumph in Egypt, and the saving of a priceless ancient treasure from the sands, had been splashed across the tabloids to excess. His pure white nose and throat, set in a dark tabby face were striking, and his flashing eyes, when set on yours, seemed to penetrate your very soul.

With a nod to the soldier to his left, whose grin denoted his better acquaintance with the tabloids, Toby leaned in closer to the butler and whispered loudly, "The Prince did suggest it was a matter of some...delicacy?" The butlercat coughed and folded up the note.

"Yes. You were expected. You had better follow me. He will be able to see you in about half an hour, just before breakfast. I checked my pocket-watch and rolled a despairing eye at Toby. It was almost noon! We were left to wait in a plush red velvet chamber, set about with a variety of glossy oak furnishings and dusted with gold brocade. One other cat, a supplicant of some kind, also awaited nervously on the Prince. A thin, tabby tom, his ribs showing beneath once-sleek fur, he grinned anxiously at us and nodded, as if to say that he waited to see a Prince every day. He was sent in before us, but could have been there no longer than five minutes, before he went away, twisting his hat in his hands as if to wring its neck. Then we were called through. Prince Hector was finishing his instructions to a valet as we arrived in the room.

"And see that Fairpaw doesn't bother me again. There is no reason for him to call here; if it's money he wants, Grimes will know if it's owed. Though for his insolence in troubling me I'm not inclined to pay him anyway! Ha!" he laughed at his own joke, and then, spotting Hunter, he brushed the valet out of the room, declaring

"Now see that I am not disturbed. I will speak to Mr Hunter - and ah? "

"Surgeon Gentlepaw" I advised

"Yes, and to the Surgeon, for some little while and then I shall finally get to my breakfast! Check those eggs are properly hot this time!"

"Your Royal Highness," began Hunter. "Oh bother all that," declared the Prince, "you had better call me Hector. Everyone does, you know! Sit down won't you! Give a cat an ulcer pacing around like that!"

We sat, precipitately, and surveyed the room. It had the character of a dressing room, in a glossy purple cast, yet its size was greater than the total space of Toby's London apartment.

"I imagine, your Highness, that 'everyone' who calls you Hector may be rather better acquainted with yourself than we are, if not indeed related to yourself. At any rate, I hope you will forgive a little shyness and a lack of pace to adopt informal protocols."

Prince Hector waved a conciliatory paw. Toby had no doubt rightly judged that this invitation to gross familiarity was not intended to be accepted.

"You got my note, then? How good a detective are you?"

"Good enough to suppose, your Highness, that the friend you refer to may not be far from this room; and that his difficulty may involve - a young lady?"

"Ha! Well, that's not difficult to guess, I suppose. You know about my engagement?"

"Of course. Our congratulations, Your Highness."

"Hem, well, had to be done, I suppose. She's a good little cat, at any rate. More than I deserve, no doubt. But - yes, as you have guessed, a small difficulty is in my way. Purest nonsense, really, but awkward. Dashed awkward."

"Another lady?"

"An actress and dancer, so she calls herself, anyway. I wrote some letters a few years ago. I had thought it all forgotten, but not long after my engagement was announced, she wrote to me."

"Threatening...?"

"Nothing so crude. She sent me her hearty congratulations!"

"But the fact and the timing of her letter…?"

"Reminded me, of course, as she had intended, that I had once written to her."

Toby stared at the ceiling, and a short silence fell. The ceiling was indeed rather remarkable. It was covered in a fresco of prancing tigers and birds, lost in a jungle, which must have taken some months to execute.

"Your Highness, I am still at somewhat of a loss - if it is a matter of money?"

"You don't understand - she hasn't yet asked for money. She means to hold this over my head until the worst possible moment." Prince Hector jumped up and scratched angrily at the windowframe. "I don't know quite what she intends to allege - but my letters were indiscreet. Foolish. It is a nuisance, perhaps an embarrassment. Princess Alexandrina's family would perhaps view it in an unhelpful light. They are rather severe people. What to you and I might seem a simple youthful indiscretion…?"

Toby nodded, thoughtfully.

"Anyway, I want the letters back. Nothing else will do - they must be destroyed."

"Very well, your Highness, you wish me to recover these documents?"

"Dead or alive!" grinned Prince Hector. "I don't much care how you do it, I don't need to see them again. But I do want to be certain the letters are gone. That I won't be troubled. Right then, breakfast time, I think." He rang a bell on a side table, and a valet approached. "Grimes will give you all the details."

"But your Highness?" Toby paused, "The lady's name?"

Prince Hector looked vexed. "Grimes can deal with you now, I tell you. Don't bother me again. The lady is Lucinda Lexington."

3

THE WICKED ACTRESS

Miss Lucinda Lexington was something of a legend to those in the theatrical know; she had been performing as part of a large troupe of dancing and singing cats, mostly female, at the Red Windmill on the outskirts of Brighton for the last three years. She was star of the show, as well as a dancer, a remarkable singer and actress. She was also athletic, performing an ingenious sort of balletic dance, of her own invention.

I had heard, of course, the rumours that she had a string of famous admirers, in the first circles of society. The 'Daily Mews' which I occasionally scanned on my visits to my sister's house, did not outright name them, but hinted in the clearest way possible without legal risk. A Member of His Majesty's Opposition had been 'tilting at windmills', a greyhaired judge was 'taking a keen interest in the seaside ballet' and so on. Miss Lexington's fame had come in no small part because of her beauty. She was an extraordinary creature. Her pale cream fur was tinged with gold, which seemed to catch light when shot through by the sun. Her large green eyes winked with fire, and her long dark lashes swept and fluttered like butterflies as she talked. I think I can be forgiven for admitting that it was some ten minutes after our arrival in her chambers before I could find a sensible word to say.

"You must forgive my companion, Miss Lexington," smiled Toby, " He is a fan of the theatre, and somewhat starstruck."

Lucinda smiled demurely. Our request for a meeting had been granted easily, and we were at our ease in a small feminine sitting room, delicately appointed with smart antique furniture, fashionably glossed in bright white paint, and liberally scattered with green and orange cushions. The apartment was on the top floor of a bright white block of ancient houses, in a classical style, that lined the seafront to the east of town. The building itself seemed intended as a setting for Lucinda's beauty.

"I cannot think, however, Mr Hunter, that you would have troubled yourself to come so far from London only for my autograph?" she said.

Toby nodded, seriously. "I fear, Miss..."

"Oh do call me Lucinda, please - if you will be Toby to me?"

"I fear that I have some unpleasant business to conduct."

"I see. Which of my very foolish admirers has been so extravagant as to engage the country's best private detectives to reason with me?"

Toby looked at her steadily, and said nothing.

"Oh Toby, surely not - the Prince?"

"Lucinda, he suggested that there might have been some - letter, or letters, of a youthful, foolish nature, which in his new position he might wish to be certain were destroyed."

"I see - and what has that to do with me?

"Miss Lexington!" I intervened, having finally recovered my voice. "We are speaking of our future King! You cannot wish..."

"Really, Robbie, you too must call me Lucinda! What cannot I wish? These young bucks, they come here, they amuse themselves by flirting with me, they parade me at the dance hall, they think it fun to write passionate letters, and then - ha! Real life intervenes, and they cast aside their amusement like a childish toy. I am to be satisfied with the trinkets they leave behind."

She caught up a handful of sparkling jewels from a bowl and cast them to the floor in front of our feet, as she leapt up to her full height. "I am not a toy! Gentlemen, I am not a toy!" Lucinda's passion had cast me dumb again. She was at her most beautiful in her seeming rage. Toby however was not fooled.

"But I think, Miss Lexington, that as you have just illustrated, you understand this game very well. So how do you propose to amuse yourself by it, if as you say, these 'trinkets' are not enough for you. He picked up a particularly large emerald from the rug and threw it back to her. She caught it, and purred appreciatively. Toby applauded, and she gave a graceful curtsey.

"Forgive me, Toby. An actress, you know, is always tempted to perform!" Toby smiled ruefully, thinking, no doubt of his own temperamental actress friend Gertie, who could certainly be so relied upon.

Lucinda sat again and dropped the gem back into the bowl. "Well, the Prince need have no concerns" she smiled. "Perhaps I have already destroyed his letters."

"I hardly think you would have done that?"

"Why not? When he abandoned me so cruelly?" But she said this last with a grin denoting no concern at all.

"Truly, Toby he need have no fears for my indiscretion. I have other fish to fry!"

"But you will not hand them over?" She shrugged. "Why should I? A cat cannot forever be leaping and singing for a living. Perhaps one day I shall require a little pension and at that time..."

"I see. They are your insurance policy. But what if the Prince could promise you such a little pension now. Could we not persuade you to part with them?"

"Do you think I would be wise to do so? Cheques can be stopped. Well I can see that this little matter troubles him quite out of proportion." She caught up another of the gems and twisted the two over and over against one another in her paw. "Perhaps - if he cares to be done with it now, I might part with them for a little fee. Just enough to ease the ache in my heart."

She scribbled a figure on a small silver clawbook and passed it to Toby. He clicked his teeth disapprovingly and passed it to me. The figure she had named was astronomical and absurd.

Toby remonstrated. "I think you know that the Prince could not obtain such a sum without recourse to his father. Have you really so little respect that you would wish to blackmail the King?" Lucinda laughed, got up, and went to the fireplace where, despite the blazing heat, the remains of a small fire burned. She reached in and pulled out the scorched remnants of a letter, of which only a few words could be deciphered, and passed it to Toby.

"There," she said carelessly, "Is the Prince's last letter. Will you give me a twopence for it?"

I jumped up and exclaimed crossly, " You have burned it while we spoke?"

She giggled. "I may be a flirt but I am not heartless! I'm afraid it was irresistible to play along with you gentlemen, in my forced role as the wicked blackmailer, but I cannot keep up such nonsense for long without a script!"

"Then you never intended blackmail?"

"No such thing! Hector is a fat fool, and he was due a fright, so I wrote to him when I heard of his engagement, but I am not a monster, and the theatre pays quite nicely enough."

Toby took the scrap of letter and folded it away carefully inside his own clawbook.

"Well then I thank you Miss Lexington and we shall take up no more of your time."

She smiled and bobbed her tail with just a hint of mockery. "Oh I needed the amusement. Brighton is so frightfully hot and predictable in June."

We left with no little sense of embarrassment.

"You are certain, I suppose that this is in fact the Prince's letter?"

"I rather think so," said Toby. "Miss Lexington is full of mischief, but not wickedness. But I hope she will take care. Her sense of humour may lead her into real trouble one day."

As we passed down the narrow stairs, a cat with a high collar and his hat pulled well down was heading up. He jostled us slightly and grumbled a word of apology whilst hurrying on, but he passed by too quickly for us to notice his face.

"A hot day for such dress." I observed. Toby looked after him thoughtfully, but all that could be seen was a dark flicking tail, disappearing inside the door of Lucinda's apartment.

"It was too hot for a fire, too. But I had not noticed it. Perhaps it is just as well Robbie that we are here. Since our commission is achieved, we can take a little holiday."

But our holiday was about to be cut short.

4

A HORRIBLE DISCOVERY

I awoke the next day to discover a note pushed under the door of my hotel room.

'Meet me at Lucinda's apartment - Toby'

I could not imagine what had occurred to make our immediate return imperative, but hailed a dogcart and rushed there straight away. It was just after eight 'o' clock and the holiday town was still waking up. The streets were quiet and my trip was fast. Toby was waiting at the bottom of the stairs, speaking to a town watch-cat, in the distinctive blue cape.

"What is it?" I demanded. Toby shook his head sadly.

"I have failed very badly, Robbie. We must set this straight."

"She had kept a letter?"

"I wish it were that" he said. "Come on, let us go up, you can see for yourself."

We tripped quickly back up the stairs to Lucinda's apartment. The door was open, apparently forced.

"A burglary?" I gasped. "But surely..." As we went in I saw the true horror of the matter. Lucinda lay dead on the floor.

I was struck silent. Toby looked quietly with me for a moment. She had been strangled, the black ribbon left tight around her throat, the end fluttering on the floor. Her glassy green eyes were stuck open as if staring in disbelief at her attacker. A single drop of blood had trickled out of her left nostril and congealed on the floor.

"Toby, I ... I am so sorry." I said.

"I see you agree with me, Robbie. This is my fault. I saw the danger, but I did not think it so close. Well, I know better now."

Toby attempted a careless manner but I could tell he was hurt and angry at himself. He crouched down by the body and spoke softly to himself, or to the departed soul.

"I will avenge you."

Then he looked up at me, and spoke briskly.

"Well, doctor, what is your diagnosis?" I gave him a cautious look then also crouched down by the body. Lucinda's golden fur fluttered in a breeze from an open window. I examined the body carefully. "There is no other sign of violence than this ligature", so saying I motioned to the ribbon. "and I cannot spot any obvious broken bones. I think she has been dead at least eight hours. A sudden attack I would say. A surprise. Perhaps she knew her assailant?"

"I should think so." said Toby, grimly.

"And you, detective?" I asked, trying to snap him out of this angry mood. "What clues have you found?" Toby jumped up and paced to the window.

"This, for one" he said. "The window was not open last night when we left. I noticed that much at least. There has been some attempt to cast this as a burglary. There is disorder in the room, and Lucinda's gems are missing."

"Then you think it was not a jewel theft gone wrong?"

"The gems were good, but not worth a murder charge. No, this is exactly what I feared but had not acted upon. She toyed with her admirers for fun, and one of them has not enjoyed the game, but decided to stop her mouth for good. Then, there is this." Toby lifted up Lucinda's limp right forepaw from the rug. A few bright threads were caught in the claws.

"She fought." he said, and gently pulled loose the threads, tucking them away in a clawpad. He shook himself and arched his back then prowled away to the desk under the window. Flicking a glance briefly behind him, he pulled at the centre drawer.

"Locked." he observed, tersely.

Toby reached inside his jacket and pulled out a small black leather pouch, which he laid carefully on the clear desk. He pulled loose a leather tie, then unrolled the pouch to reveal a set of small tools that put me in mind of my own surgical instruments.

"What on earth...?" I demanded.

Toby had already selected one of the tools and applied it to the lock. A turn to the left, a push, a turn to the right and with a sharp click the drawer popped open. Inside was a neat pile of letters bound with blue ribbon, another pile of photographs bound in red, and a small silver notebook. Toby riffled quickly through the letters, his eyes widening a little at some passages, then tossed them over to me. The photographs he similarly scanned and tossed aside, with a hiss, then seized the notebook and curled up with it on the sofa. I examined the letters. Reader, what follows may shock you. Although the passage of time has made some cats immune from taint and scandal, this tale cannot be told without revealing that some highly respected and eminent persons of our time were entangled with ladies of the underworld of Brighton. Lucinda was perhaps one of the more respectable cats of her type, but nonetheless except for young cats-about-town it cannot have been a matter of pride to have such a connection revealed. For others it would have meant disaster and disgrace. To some extent this is true still. So where it has been expedient to do so, I have hidden some identities in this tale behind an alias. Still, I can tell you that the correspondence in my hand included letters from a High Court Judge and a Bishop, of a nature that would have appalled their contemporaries, and had the latter stripped of his collar! I was interrupted in my fascinated perusal by a sharp sniff from Toby. I looked up to see him fixing down a page in front of him with an exposed claw.

"Here we have it!" my friend declared.

"What?"

"If I mistake not, our list of suspects. Though it will take a little deciphering."

He threw over the notebook to me, and I turned back to the marked page. I could make nothing of it. There were four rows of letters, and next to each a series of numbers. I reproduce the list below.

JP 4-1 1-2 1-3 5-4 3-5 7-6

BR 7-1 21-1 4-2 18-2 4-3 20-5

HrH 12-1 14-1 15-1 17-`1 19-1 25-1 16-2

RtHn 4-3 15-3 16-3 22-3 23-3 29-3 5-4 12-4 24-5 31-5

"Well?" asked Toby with a grin.

"Some sort of ... ah - is it betting odds?

"Something like it!" he chuckled. "You find it suggestive, I am sure?"

"Yes" I replied, doubtfully.

"Never mind, all will become clear. I shall explain it to you over lunch." Clearly the little puzzle had cheered him somewhat. "Come, we had best be away before the police surgeon castigates us for trampling on the evidence."

"What about all the letters?" I asked. "Put them back. And I had better relock the drawer. Bishop Redfur would not like his honeyed phrases to be shared outside this apartment."

"Indeed not!" I agreed fervently. "What of the photographs?"

Toby cocked his head to one side in thought, then snatched up the packet again, rifling through whilst muttering under his breath, "I think there was just one that...yes, here it is, aha!" he said, pulling out a blurred snapshot. "I have copied the numbers into my own clawpad for reference, though I think their significance is already clear to me. They may prove useful nonetheless" he mused.

Then tossing the notebook back into the drawer beside the packet of letters and the photographs, he relocked it carefully, and replaced the pick-like tool in its case.

"What about the other photograph?" I asked

"I shall mention it to the local police in due course, once I am certain of my facts. This is a rather more delicate matter than I had imagined Robbie - it involves not only Royalty but also the Law, Religion and ... Politics!"

"Politics?" I echoed.

"I fear so." Toby replied, handing me the snapshot. It was a somewhat blurred picture of a group of young to middle-aged cats grouped smiling around the coy-looking Lucinda, who looked directly into the camera. The two nearest to her had a paw each on her shoulders. It was not compromising but perhaps made them look a little too familiar with such an actress. For many cats this would have been embarrassing at worst. For the cat with his face turned in open admiration towards Lucinda, it was more than that. The crowd about her were all Members of

Parliament, and the cat to her right was a leading member of the Shadow Cabinet.

5
NUMBERS

Once back in our hotel, I demanded some explanation of Toby.

"What is this cipher? The letters and numbers, can they be translated?"

"I think we can read a great deal from them." he nodded.

"They are a code, then?"

"Hardly so much as that. The information they conceal is bland enough in itself - if somewhat damning."

"I see" I said. "At least, no I don't, curse it all. Great Bast take it, Toby, do explain properly, won't you?"

Hunter sighed and set down his newspaper.

"You saw of course that the letters represented some of Lucinda's - ah - clientele. Her closest admirers."

"Um, yes" I muttered. Though I had seen nothing of the kind. Toby took pity on me.

"HrH is clearly Prince Hector. His Royal Highness. You see?"

"Oh!" I gaped. Then BR?" He nodded. "Bishop Redfur. And JP I suspect to be Judge Pennyclaw. There was a letter from him, was there not?"

"There was a letter signed 'Penny'. But..."

"I know! The great Pennyclaw, terror of the benches, to write such drivel! Still, we would need more proof than that to make a case ourselves!"

"So then RtHn is Right Honourable. A Member of Parliament in fact."

"Precisely, Robbie, Bravo!"

"But ...which one? Surely not Daniel Alleyfeather?"

"Why not? You can see his mooning face staring at her in the picture - probably taken at last year's party conference, when the Opposition were here. They stayed at the Grand Hotel did they not? I assume that some of the younger crowd attended one of the Red Windmill shows in the evening and this was taken afterwards. But RtHn could be another of the MPs in this picture."

"Yes I see. But - what are the numbers then?"

I wonder if you have guessed, reader, for I had not.

JP 4-1 1-2 1-3 5-4 3-5 7-6

BR 7-1 21-1 4-2 18-2 4-3 20-5

HrH 12-1 14-1 15-1 17-`1 19-1 25-1 16-2

RtHn 3-3 15-3 16-3 22-3 23-3 29-3 5-4 12-4 24-5 31-5 34

"Have you a calendar handy, Robbie?" sighed Toby. I pulled out my diary and turned to the small calendar at the rear. "The fourth of January this year was a Friday, was it not?" I found the relevant month and scanned the column.

"You do know the strangest things, Toby" I chuckled. "But what on earth has that to do with..." "As was the first of February I believe - and therefore the first of March also. Can you see it now?"

"I ... oh!" As I scanned between the diary page and the list of numbers, a pattern swam into view.

"Ah, well it's obvious now. They are dates of course!"

"Of course" muttered Toby with a munificent wave.

"But what do they tell you?"

"They are the dates when... when Lucinda met with the cats on this list!" I exclaimed with sudden insight.

"Quite so" muttered Toby with a yawn. "But surely you can see more than that?"

"Ah - no, sorry but I don't."

"Very well then, I shall tell you my deductions. Simply observe the pattern of the dates. What are the days of the week, at what frequency do the meetings occur? From this we can readily deduce something about the mind that made the appointments."

"So? What do you read from them?"

Toby held out a paw and ticked off our suspects on his claws.

"The Judge was a creature of habit - his liaisons with Lucinda he regarded in the way of a small monthly treat to himself. He had no grand passion for her. The Bishop has struggled with his conscience somewhat. He knew the meetings to be inappropriate and briefly was winning the struggle - no meeting after the beginning of March you see? But then this month he has succumbed again! The Prince enjoyed himself immensely and then tired of the amusement by February. In this, as in other things, he was a glutton and sickened himself. But the Right Honourable whoever was smitten from the start, coming as often as he could when free from Parliamentary business on Fridays and Saturdays. I imagine, if it be comfort to your injured sense of propriety, Robbie, that he is not a married cat."

"Come to think of it none of them are. Lucinda had her principles" I observed.

"Indeed so, even if none of these rogues did."

"So - one of them did it you think?"

"It would seem likely, given Lucinda's idea of a joke, that she has pressed at least one of these cats with the threat of embarrassment a little too far, with disastrous results."

"But which one? I suppose at least we can rule out the Prince himself?"

"Ah, but that is just what we cannot do" Toby tutted, and paced fretfully around the room. "He is gluttonous but not stupid. We know that Lucinda had taunted him. If he had planned to eliminate for good this threat to his impending marriage, he could have involved us precisely with the idea of excluding himself from suspicion."

"Sounds like a very foolish plan to me."

"Well," said Toby "Indeed so, I don't think it likely. But it is too soon to say he is in the clear. If he has an obvious and very public alibi for last night, I shall be so much more concerned."

"But," I flustered "a Judge, a Bishop, an MP - surely, none of them could have murdered?"

"I agree we are in some difficulty!" Toby laughed. "I think we shall do very well if we come out of this matter without causing great offence to His Majesty's benches, the Royal Family, the Government or to Great Bast himself!"

"What shall we do then? Which of them is most likely?"

Toby looked sober. "From his regular habits I deduce a highly logical turn of mind in the Judge. As unlikely as it may seem, I think he should be our first port of call, followed by the Bishop."

"And what about our Right Honourable Suspect?"

"We had better set about quickly finding him a name. If it is Alexander, it will be well known. The hallowed halls of Westminster are a byword for gossip. But I fear it may well be the case. Lucinda has not troubled to keep a register for all her admirers, of whom there were doubtless more than four. I am certain that a mere junior MP would be of no interest to her." He smiled broadly. "Before that, though, I fear we must torment ourselves by risking the ruin of our characters."

"What do you mean?"

"I think we had best be better informed and get some evidence of our suspicions before visiting any of these eminent characters. Robbie my dear friend, I fear we must visit the most notorious cabaret show in Brighton!"

6
THE RED WINDMILL

We set off that very evening intent on a visit to the infamous Red Windmill. The Windmill itself is impossibly ancient in origin, of Yooman times, but overlaid with so much repair and gaslight signage, whilst hedged with so many restaurants, bars and hotels that its original pastoral occupants would fail to recognise it. It is set high on a coastal hill, facing out to sea, with the town of Brighton some miles off to the west and the small village of Rottingdean in the valley just to the east. The mill retains its sails, but they have long since ceased to turn, being fixed in the shape of an X. It is tall and black, with a large door cut in one side at the base. Inside it is much larger than apparent from outside, as one descends cut stone steps to a large cabaret theatre, with round tables set out across the room, in front of an opulent stage. The stage itself was set with thick red curtains, tied with gold rope, and the floor below painted red - leading to the nickname for the theatre which had later stuck. The whole of this room was dug out at least a hundred years ago by the original impresario of the theatre. I fear I must admit to a sneaking sense of excitement as evening approached. The dancing cats of the Windmill are notorious for good reason; their show is said to be quite unforgettable. I rather looked forward at least to this part of our visit. We took a table to one side of the room, about halfway between the entrance and the stage. We were fairly early, and a lone singer, plain in looks but with stunning blue-grey fur gently filled the air with soulful tunes. Toby looked about him as the tables filled and I quietly perused the menu. It was long on drinks and short on substance.

Toby shot me a sympathetic glance. "Ah but there is plenty of food for the soul, Robbie"

The singer concluded one song to a gentle ripple of applause, then nodded to the pianist, who was joined by a small band of other players, trumpets and strings. They picked up the tempo with a brightly jaunty tune, and the singer raised her voice and began to sway.

"Do you know who will appear tonight?" I asked Toby who shook his head.

"The loss of Lucinda will have thrown their usual schedules into disarray. Still I imagine these theatrical types are not unused to sudden confusion. No doubt the Ribbon Dancers will still perform. And of course La Chanteuse is still with us." He gestured to the singer now completing her set.

"What, her?" I spluttered, astonished. "That is La Chanteuse? Why she is nothing like the posters!"

"One cannot draw a voice. You must admit, her songs pull at the heart."

"Yes, of course - but it's misleading! Why in the portraits advertising the Windmill in London, she is..."

"Beautiful? Do you expect honesty in an advertisement?"

"I suppose not," I grumbled. "I hope at least the Dancers are... somewhat as advertised."

"Beauty is in the eye of the beholder, Robbie." Toby remonstrated. "But I am sure you will find their 'astonishing acrobatics' quite as promised."

The compere, 'Dicky' Bowpaws now came to the stage and garnered some more emphatic applause for La Chanteuse before handing her down into the wings.

"Good evening ladies and gentlecats," he began. "Welcome one and all to the Red Windmill. I regret that I must open this evening's show with some very sad news, as we have learned today that the star of our show, the wonderful Lucinda Lexington, has met with a terrible accident, and will not be able to join us. We shall miss her terribly. In her place this evening, her regular understudy Miss Victoria Gingersnap will do her brave best to dance on. I know she will have your best wishes. But we begin, as ever, with the astonishing Ribbon Dancers!"

The band struck up once more and played a fast Spanish tune, as the curtain pulled back. Ten black and white cats, each wielding a colourful ribbon, ran onto the stage and began to dance. I can truly say that their performance is astonishing. Each wore a headdress of some sparkling gold material resembling a crown, and their fur shone like glass. The ribbons danced in the air in mimicry of the tumblers below, and they jumped and leapt and ran about forming hearts, diamonds and on one occasion the semblance of a face in the air above them. After a pair of 'comical' cats who amused me not at all, it was the turn of Victoria Gingersnap. She was quite beautiful; her marmalade colouring and ice-blue eyes were set off by a delicate elfin figure. She opened her performance with a bow first to the company at tables below, a wave at the few gentry in high boxes to the side of the stage, then a kiss blown into the air, with the whispered word, 'Lucinda'. Then she began to dance. It was extraordinary; her balletic moves suggested the flight of a swan through the air, or a colt galloping through the fields. Finally she danced a leaping, triumphant dance of joy, concluding with a series of spinning pirouettes, which flung out her green cape into a circle about her neck as she turned. She bowed and left the stage. The compere announced the interval and we leapt up, headed backstage. We were naturally paused in this objective by the compere Dicky himself.

"Can I assist you gentlecats? Something ... or someone you wanted to see?" I didn't much like his tone, but still we needed his help.

"We wish to speak to the performers regarding the death of Lucinda Lexington." I said.

"Hush! Not so loud!" he complained. "Are you with the police? They have already been here and got nothing out of it."

"I am Toby Hunter" said that great cat. "And I am here in a private capacity. I am sure you would want everything possible done to catch the assailant of your beloved star."

"Yes, well, no doubt." said Dicky. "Perhaps you'd better speak to the manager."

"Certainly" said Toby. "And who would that be?" Dicky laughed heartily and gestured to a small grey door in the wall.

"Be my guest" he invited. We stepped inside and the door snapped closed behind us - it appeared to be locked. A small winding staircase led up and up until we could see lights out of small windows cut in the wall.

"I think we are inside the windmill itself!" I hissed at Toby. He nodded and pressed on up the stairs until we came out into a small office, laid out in these ancient surroundings with surprisingly modern furnishings. A neat square desk was in the centre of the room, and curled up on the far side of it was an greying old mollie.

She opened one eye, then the other and glared at us crossly.

"What do you want?" she said.

"Madam, we were looking for the manager. Dicky suggested that..."

"Oh he does like his joke" she growled, uncurling herself and stretching out. "I am the manager of the Red Windmill." She scratched lazily at the paperwork piled on the desk and rang a small brass handbell. A maid poked a nervous set of whiskers around the door.

"Yes, Miss Redclaw?" she said.

"Tea" demanded Miss Redclaw. "For three, I suppose. Be quick about it."

I was more than a little taken aback. Of course in our modern world many professions are now open to the ladies, but still I balked at a female managing this kind of business. It seemed rather indelicate. Still, as Miss Redclaw eyed us narrowly over her steaming cup of tea, I admitted privately to myself that she was no trembling flower.

"You may go, Mittens" she nodded to the maid, then gave us both a final appraising glance before turning to Toby. "About Lucinda, then?"

He nodded gravely.

"I have already spoken to the police... but you know that, don't you Mr Hunter."

We had not introduced ourselves and I started at this. Toby seemed untroubled. "Yes Miss Redclaw, and may I introduce my associate Surgeon Gentlepaw?"

She dipped lightly in an approximation of a nosegreeting, without stirring from her seat.

"We spoke to Miss Lexington on another matter only yesterday, she was most helpful, and I feel some professional obligation to - take an interest shall we say?"

"You have your pride no doubt" said Redclaw, drolly.

"Indeed"

"What do you want of me? She was a performer here - do you think her death was connected with that in some way?"

"I don't know" said Toby. "I intend to find out and to catch her killer."

"Ha! Well you intend more than the police then. They intend, I rather think, to ensure that the matter will not trouble any of the very eminent personages that it might. I am rather surprised that that is not your purpose Mr Hunter - surely you represent one of the most eminent personages of all?" She gave him a sly stare and took another sip of tea.

"How would you know of our connection there?"

"Oh every palace needs cooks and cleaners - and they tend to be underpaid. Don't look so shocked Surgeon. It is very much in my line of business to keep abreast of fashionable society."

Toby stood up. "Madam can you help us or not?"

"I believe I could, Mr Hunter, if you could give me a good reason to do it."

He thought for a moment, pacing the room then looked back at her, as she sat very still and unblinking in her chair.

"I believe you were once a singer here, Miss Redclaw?"

She looked surprised. "Before your time, my dear, yes, I was."

"Then perhaps you will have some compassion - some feeling - for your employees. In any case it cannot be good for business to have them killed off? I can only assure you that whoever my employer may have been up until this morning, I now consider myself at the service of the late Lucinda Lexington. I intend to find her killer. Will you help me?"

Redclaw gave one slow blink of her eyes, then opened a drawer in her desk, and pulled out a sleek black clawbook. She flicked quickly through it to find the right page and looked up.

"If you can give me two of the names on this list I shall give you the rest."

"Very well then" said Toby. "Prince Hector and Bishop Redfur."

She nodded "Pennyclaw and Alleyfeather." She snapped shut her book and stood up. "If there was nothing else?"

Toby held up a paw.

"Just one thing. Is there anyone here who might have had reason to hate her? Any - shall we say - professional jealousy?"

Redclaw smiled for the first time since we had met her. A small, thin, slow smile that entirely failed to reach her eyes.

"Well I'm sure you will find her colleagues all terribly sorry to lose her. But then actresses and performers do tend to be good at playing a role, don't they? Surely I don't need to tell a detective to consider who benefits? Good day to you both."

It was our cue to leave. We took it.

7

RIBBONS AND BELLS

We found our way back to the cabaret area quite easily, and saw the crowd already thinning. Dicky was leading rounds of failing applause for the various performers. Victoria got the strongest volume of appreciation, perhaps in sympathy for filling in at short notice. We hung back as the last of the audience filed out through the doors, and the performers began to gather at a few of the tables nearest the stage. Some kitchen staff brought out plates of food to them, and 'Buttons' from the comic duo of 'Buttons and Bells' got in a round of drinks. The performers began to relax, the females had mostly taken off head-dresses and thrown on plain dressing gowns over their sparkling costumes. A buzz of conversation had just begun when we approached and Toby coughed gently to announce our presence.

"Show's over, gents" said Dicky, standing up.

"And these ladies are off duty, as you can see." He had quite dropped his jovial manner. Then he peered at us more closely and chuckled.

"Oh you two again! You got little change from old Lady Scratch then?"

"Oh don't Dicky! She'll hear you!" wailed one of the Ribbon dancers.

"On the contrary, Miss Redclaw was most helpful" said Toby. "She also suggested that Lucinda's fellow performers might help to shed a little light on matters."

I gasped, hopefully unnoticed, at this effrontery. Dicky looked momentarily astonished, before comprehension flickered in his eyes and he nodded at Toby.

"Well it don't surprise me," he lied "Old... I mean Miss Redclaw did always have a soft spot for our Lucinda, didn't she Ginger?"

Victoria, who had followed this exchange with narrowed eyes, took up a glass of sparkling wine, and took a deliberate sip before answering only, "Yes", setting down her glass and looking away

"Excellent" said Toby, drawing up a stool, and picking up a fried sardine.

"Hungry, Robbie? Which of you knew her well then? Did she have a best friend here?"

I drew up a second stool, squeezing in between two of the Ribbon dancers, who eyed me with mock horror then burst into giggles. I took Toby's hint and filled a plate with the snacks appearing on the table - more substantial and homespun fare than available to the regular clientele. Clearly he felt I could be of most use to him with my mouth full.

"She took quite a shine to you, Tinker, didn't she?" said 'Bells', whose real name was Bradley Bellringer. He had entirely dropped his jolly bantering tone and seemed in fact quite morose. I liked him much better.

Tinker was the youngest Ribbon dancer - perhaps just out of school. Her shining blue eyes seemed too big for her small face, and her large pointed ears stuck out at slightly odd angles.

"Miss Lucinda was very kind to me" she whispered. "She talked to me about when she started on the stage. She was very kind."

"I don't think that's quite what the detective wants to know" growled a gloomy Bradley, shaking his paw at her. One of his costume bells rang merrily as he did so and he pulled it off irritably, snapping the cotton. "What about her gentlecat friends?" he sneered.

Tinker looked affronted. "Lucinda had a great many fans. People wanted to meet her in person. It was flattering but she couldn't really spend much time with them all. So she had to - um - manage them."

"That's what she told you?" sniffed Bradley.

"Regulars start to think they know you, just from a stage performance." said Tinker "And then they ones that Lucinda agreed to meet - important cats that she didn't want to offend. Well they could get a little bit silly about her. And then they wouldn't like to think that she had other special friends. So she had to make sure that they didn't bump into one another - backstage, sort of thing."

Victoria hissed loudly. "Lot of nonsense. 'Fans'! Ha!"

Tinker seemed about to cry. "That's what she told me" she finished in her smallest whisper.

Bradley put a paw on her shoulder and pulled out a bright green pawkerchief, which he offered to her. "There, there" he said gruffly. "Don't take any notice of the Gingersnap. She's just jealous. Even now, Bast help her!"

He turned to Victoria and pulled out of her paw the bottle with which she had been refilling her glass. "Lucinda!" he gasped and blew a kiss into the air in mockery of her earlier performance.

Victoria looked ready to spit at him, but then turned in a moment to laughter. "Well Tinker's right about one thing anyway, Lucinda had plenty of admirers. So if I want to win them over I have to start by looking like I care, don't I!"

"You think you will remain the new 'star turn' then?" asked Toby, gently.

Victoria gave him an icy stare and smoothed back the fur from her cheeks. "Of course I will. Who else is there? I'm the only one of this lot that can really dance."

Several of the Ribbon dancers choked on their supper at this assertion, but they seemed well used to Victoria's vanity and ignored her. I dared a question.

"Tinker, just how did Lucinda manage these admirers of hers?"

Her nose flushed pink. "She had a sort of diary. Just for appointments - she showed it to me once."

"What did it look like? Can you remember?" "I can do better than that. I can show you" she said eagerly, and plucked a bright pink clawpad diary from her bag. Toby looked astonished. "That's it?" he gasped.

"Oh no!" said Tinker, embarrassed. "This one is mine. Lucinda gave it to me, when she bought hers for this year. She thought I'd like to have one the same as hers."

Bradley cuffed her gently, flicking her ear. "You little idiot" he said, warmly. "What do you want to go copying Lucinda for? You're better than she was anyday."

"But I can't dance like she could, nothing like it. You know that!" Tinker laughed, smiling at him.

Bradley only muttered to himself, "That's not what I meant."

I quickly swallowed my sardine and intervened, to spare his embarrassment.'Bells' had rather grown on me, despite his gruff manner. "Did any of you ever meet any of Miss Lexington's more ardent followers? Could you tell us who they were, or anything about them?"

Dicky spoke up. "We all knew who they were alright. No doubt Miss Redclaw knew best of all. But they aren't names that any of us would want to bandy about, I'm sure." He looked around the troupe, including their fast lowering eyes in his certainty.

"Well then perhaps you could at least tell us if any of them seemed more likely to kill than another!" Toby was cross. "This is, ladies and gentlecats, a murder we are speaking of. Or have you forgotten already?"

The assembled company stared at him, pawfuls of food, glasses of drink frozen on the way to mouths.

Then Richard 'Buttons' Greywhiskers spoke up. "I'll tell you that" he said in elegant tones, quite unlike the low bantering voice of his act. "The swine took a swipe at me when I tried to stop him going into Lucinda's dressing room one day."

"When was this?" asked Toby, sharply. "Oh, way back. Early April I think?"

"The fifth?"

"Could be? Say, if you already know things, why do you bother us asking them."

"I do like to have my little theories confirmed." Toby smiled. "Speaking of which, tell me this, was it Alleyfeather who swiped at you? Or Pennyclaw?"

8

THE NOBLE JUDGE

We awaited Judge Pennyclaw in his Chambers just off the Strand. Coming back to London fresh from the seaside it struck me anew what a smelly, dirty place it can be. In Brighton the salt air from the sea mingled with the tang of fresh fish. Though the town itself could be crowded, the onshore breeze constantly sweetened the streets. The Strand itself was full of the scent of cats, fresh washed and otherwise. The sharp perfume of fine linens and rosewaters from the cats briskly clipping along the street mingled with nipjuice and the stench of unkemp, matted fur seeping up from the alleyways. The forest of tall buildings spreading for miles across the city blocked any breezes, or else funnelled them into cat-made canyons, whipping them faster into blasts of powerful odour that could strike the face like a blow as you turned a corner. The harsh odour of the dogs and their carts oozed up from the road, and the sewers, though functioning better this year since Parliament's latest ruling on their use, maintained a constant background fog of ordure.

The Chambers themselves were quite pleasant. Judge Pennyclaw had the top floor suite, his private office, and an outer waiting area, in which his two clerks worked. A small seating area accommodated lawyers avid for his attention, and ourselves. Toby had secured an appointment on the pretext of a discussion on a previous case of his, where the Judge had presided over the trial earlier that year and they were now able to discuss it freely. The windows looked out over gardens, mostly laid to lawn but edged about on this fine summer day with a thick border of tall blue and green flowers. The Judge's door opened and a highly anxious young barrister exited, dropping half his papers as he did so. He continued to edge out backwards, scooping the papers back into his briefcase, and casting unhappy looks at the other barrister. This second barrister had clearly had a better time with the judge and was exchanging a joke with him as he left. The door slammed shut again and one of the clerks cast us a sympathetic glance.

"He'll be with you shortly. He just likes to take a moment between meetings. Really, they talk of the 'fallow period' in the summer, but there is no such thing. Court may not be sitting but it's the only time when the lawyers with the big cases can bother his Lordship - and don't they just take the chance. Oh!"

His Lordship was now peering out of his door, his half-moon spectacles pinched precariously close to the end of his nose, and a stern glare directed over them at his clerk. His tattered red bib of office hung loosely about his neck. Silenced, the clerk sat down again, and the Judge summoned us with a crooked claw. He shut the door behind us and I noticed that all the noise of the room outside was quite silenced. Clearly we had come to the right place for a private conversation.

"Well," began Pennyclaw, expansively. "The Red Barn case, eh? Fascinating business. I shall be quite glad of a chance to discuss it with you. Really when that new evidence was found during the trial we had hardly a moment to consider - a cat's life was at stake after all! But it did cast a completely different light on it all. And as you know young Feathersnap was never caught. I suspect he emigrated. A great many ships were sailing that week, though where he could have got the money..."

Toby interrupted. "I'm afraid, Judge Pennyclaw, that although I too should be glad to discuss the case, we may have to await a future opportunity. I know your time is in great demand, and a rather more urgent matter has arisen which I must raise with you today. It is not so much the Red Barn which has brought us to your door, as the Red Windmill."

Shock distorted Pennyclaw's features. "The Windmill?" he whispered, stricken. "But I have nothing to... I mean... She..." He collapsed into his chair, and left our drinks unpoured.

Toby took up the heavy decanter of honeysuckle brandy and poured him a drink. "I take it, your Lordship, that you had known Miss Lexington since at least the fourth of January this year - and you met fairly regularly, around the beginning of the month - until this month."

"She swore there were no records kept!"

"The lady was reasonably truthful on that point. Still a romantic soul may wish to retain a charming letter, don't you think?"

The Judge nearly choked on his brandy. "Romantic? Her? Nonsense. Not a romantic bone in her body. That's what I liked about her! Beautiful to look at of course, and I don't deny that I appreciated that, since you seem to know all about it. But she had a mind that could dance rings around most of the foolish young barristers that stumble through these doors. So she kept my letters? Well, well, I wonder what she meant by that. It wasn't attraction for my own lovely self I assure you!"

The Judge got up and paced over to arch a claw at a photograph of himself, posed snugly beside the Prime Minister, taken on the day of his appointment to the High Court. "This was more like it, I daresay. Clever molly, she was. She liked to know the people that mattered. I had promised her an introduction one day. He couldn't have gone there - to the Windmill - of course. But I thought perhaps, some discreet restaurant in town. Still - we shall never know now."

"Indeed so. Whatever Lucinda's plans, they will never come to anything. " Toby spoke bitterly. "However you might care to explain why the delightful Miss Lexington was obliged to observe your Honour exchanging such harsh words, if not blows, with a member of His Majesty's Parliament?"

"Who told you that?" growled the Judge.

"Is it true?"

"In my profession, Mister Hunter, and I should have thought often in yours, we are concerned less with what is true, than what can be proved."

Toby merely widened his eyes and lengthened his stare.

"Very well then, yes, I did have the uncomfortable experience of an altercation with - a certain young MP. Young idiot I should say. I mean really, did he think he was the only cat capable of amusing Miss Lexington in a private audience? He seemed most put out that I was there. The poor molly had been distracted by a sore tooth and most unfortunately 'double booked' us as it were. We were both expected at the same time, only I got there first! She was very gracious explaining to the poor sap once he had been calmed down."

"Alleyfeather, you mean."

"Yes."

"And it was he who had the fight with Richard Greywhiskers?"

"Who? Oh you mean the comic turn. Surprising really for such a comical chap, that he handled himself so well in a fight. Came out without a scratch, but Alleyfeather had blood on his nose. Trouble explaining that to the Parliamentary Whip no doubt!"

"This was in April?"

"Yes. But look here - I admired the lady, enjoyed her company, and yes, I don't particularly want that broadcast about. A Judge is supposed to be more - ah - sober - in his habits. But why would I kill her, eh? I'm no romantic fool. And I'm too close to retirement to care that much about a little scandal. Look a bit closer at someone who couldn't stand for it, that's my advice. And now, gentlecats, I fear my next appointment is rather overdue. If you will excuse me?"

We were hurriedly ushered out, and another set of anxious-looking barristers ushered in.

"Could it have been him?" I begged of Toby as we crossed the lawns below the offices.

"I can't see it, Robbie. It begins to look bleak for young Alleyfeather though. Motive and a temper. We had better see him next."

9
THE PRIVATE OFFICE

The administration necessary to the life of a Parliamentarian is quite extraordinary in its extent. A Government Minister of course, besides his Departmental office staff, will have political advisers, and a small office space maintained in the Houses of Parliament in Westminster. The opposition has not quite such a luxurious position (one reason I suppose why they are always so desperate for power), but Shadow Ministers will still likely retain a private office in the Party offices, as well as their Parliamentary base. It was telling therefore that Daniel Alleyfeather wished to meet us in neither of these offices, but instead in St James' Park, by the bridge over the great lake.

"Rather melodramatic, don't you think?" Toby chided him. "Surely a Member of Parliament may meet a public figure without too much comment."

Unexpectedly, Danny laughed out loud. "Too much comment? You don't know very much about Parliament then Mr Hunter! Why the place is fuelled by gossip. We eat it and drink it and breathe it. Ten seconds after any other MP saw me talking to you there would be fifteen different appalling rumours circulating the building. At least here I can claim that I bumped into you by chance. I often come here to feed the ducks."

As if to prove this last point he extracted a paper bag from his briefcase and began to scatter crumbs down onto the lake. We were shortly surrounded by a fearful crowd of quacking and flapping birds, too numerous to count.

"And do you suppose, Mr Alleyfeather, that any such rumours would be worse than the truth of it?" I was piqued by his apparently casual treatment of our serious mission, but I soon regretted my comment at his gentlecatly reaction.

He sobered up abruptly. "Well Surgeon, I am so ashamed of the whole business that I'm sure I deserve some embarrassment at the very least. But I need some time. I have a prominent position and I have let down my party. I should like to try to find a way to lessen the harm before the vultures, and Bast help me, the press are let loose. Shall we stroll? There's a delightful little cafe just across the bridge."

Alleyfeather strode confidently to the cafe and sat at an outside table, his eyes fixed on the lake. He was a lean, marmalade-coloured cat, with a long, slim nose, and rounded ears. His fur was lightly slicked with some scentless pomade, and a neat orange necktie circled his throat. We joined him, and observed the passing crowds for a moment. It was a fine day, and there was a striking contrast between the rushing civil servants, taking no notice of their surroundings, mothers exercising their kits, and dawdling lovers, admiring the flowers. He began without prompting.

"I first met Lucinda Lexington, as you must have guessed, at the party conference in March. Did you ever see her dance?"

Toby nodded, "Once - some years ago."

"You understand then, she was quite captivating. Like no one else. Afterwards - I - asked to meet her." Lost in thought, he clawed at his own necktie, as if it had tightened around his throat.

"With what intention?" Alleyfeather looked around for the first time from his survey of the lake. "Must you go into all this ... no don't bother I understand of course that you must. Only - it seems so sordid."

"Murder is not a pleasant business."

His mouth tightened and he looked away. "Murder" he whispered.

"Indeed, Mr Alleyfeather. So we had better hear it all. We may be able to eliminate you from the enquiry. There are a number of possible suspects. But we cannot do so without hearing the truth."

"Well then," he stood up, abruptly. "The truth is that I loved her! What do you think of me now?"

"I am very sorry for you," said Toby. "But do sit down. You cannot help yourself or her by making a scene. And I thought you wanted to preserve your privacy?"

"Ha!" Alleyfeather laughed bitterly. "Well, you will understand from my admission just now what a great fool I have been. I loved Lucinda, I fell quite hopelessly in love from the first moment I saw her. I wanted to see her all the time. To be with her every moment of every day."

"I imagine the demands on your time as Shadow Chancellor got in the way of that somewhat," said Toby drolly.

"You mock me? I suppose I must get used to that. She was kind to me, she saw me as often as she could."

"When she was not busy with someone else?" I asked mildly.

Danny turned to me and hissed with rage. "Do not sully that lady's name, Surgeon."

"Yet I understand that you had a little altercation with another friend of hers? In April?" Toby asked.

Alleyfeather looked at him coldly. "You refer to my misunderstanding with Judge Pennyclaw?"

Toby spread his paws in an apologetic gesture.

"Yes, yes, you have to ask. Lucinda had explained to me, so many people wanted her time. They were influential people and she could not say no to them all. They could make life difficult for her, for her employer, if she did. So she was kind to them. It wasn't the same as with her and me. It was just - more than I could bear that day to see him with her. That ancient old Tom."

"I think that the Noble Judge would be horrified to hear himself so described. And you sustained a small injury?"

Alleyfeather made a dismissive gesture. "A tiny scratch. It was nothing."

"And then?"

"Then? Nothing - I met her a few more times, until I heard the terrible news on Monday. I was devastated."

"Not relieved?"

"What? No, of course not. Why would I be relieved?"

Toby traced a pattern in the sugar with his claw. "It was a potentially embarrassing connection, for a cat in your position. As you have acknowledged yourself, it will leave you in some difficulty even now as the facts emerge. If she had been blackmailing you...?"

Danny stood up, and threw a note down on the table. "You do not understand." he muttered.

He turned ready to walk away, but looked back and stared at us. "You have understood nothing. I loved her. I intended ... I was going to marry her."

10

THE PALACE OF BAST

Following our stunning interview with the Right Honourable Danny Alleyfeather, we had caught the next train back to the south coast, and were now on a coach heading to meet the final suspect on our list, the Bishop Redfur of Chichester. The Bishop's residence was in the grounds of the Bastian Cathedral of Chichester, so we had a fairly long and uncomfortable journey to make.

The Dog carts that ran along the south coast road at that time were owned by a large family of hounds, of sturdy body, but not one whit mechanically minded. So although our progress was rapid, it was jolting and horribly uncomfortable, for the carts were quite unsprung. There was a horse-carriage, but Toby had decreed that we could not wait for its weekly run. So there we sat, bouncing up and down in the back of a carriage through a gap in whose floor I could observe the shingled road racing along beneath. For some miles the road had been the enemy of conversation, but a smoother patch after Worthing allowed me an opening.

"You surely cannot suspect that the Bishop himself had something to do with this?"

Toby, clinging grimly with all his claws to the seat, managed a shrug. "Then who am I to suspect, Surgeon - do tell me? Is it better to suppose that a Prince, a Judge of the High Court or a Member of Parliament are lying to us? And the higher the climb up the ladder, the greater the fall. A Bishop would have every reason to wish a dalliance with an actress to be kept quiet. He would be a laughing stock."

"Yes - but murder?"

"I agree - it seems absurd. But then it does for all of them does it not? Why kill a blackmailer? Whatever embarrassment you are faced with it surely seems better than to be pursued for a capital crime. Unless it was not so calculated a crime. More a moment of unreason, of passion?"

"I cannot associate such a moment with His Reverence Bishop Redfur."

Toby chortled. "Well I shall at least enjoy seeing him explain away the connection to us. What did you think of the other two? Are either of them more likely?"

I shook my head in dismay. "The Judge I did not like, I admit. But he seemed rational and measured enough. I felt quite sorry for Alleyfeather. He was in love, and he has lost his love, and may quite likely lose his career too."

Toby nodded, "There was passion enough there."

"Yes, but because he was in love. As he said himself, why would he hurt Lucinda?"

"Politicians do not join the Cabinet, Shadow or otherwise without some degree of ruthlessness, nor some powers of dissimulation. I do not believe he was telling us the whole truth."

"But his pain seemed real."

"So it did. Not so real as Lucinda's death though. And I am sworn to find her killer."

Toby fell into a glum reverie, and I took in the view. The dog-cart followed a path roughly parallel to the sea, where a few fishing skiffs bobbed gently on the sparkling waters a mile or so out. That way, across the Channel, lay France, though it could not be seen from this distance. Ahead of us, over a few more hills, lay the city of Chichester. The surrounding countryside was lush and green, full of pleasant rolling fields with ripening crops, herds of chickens and goats corralled by watchful dogs, lounging by the field gates with one eye always open. As we approached the city the fields began to be dotted with outlying hamlets, a few dwellings clustered around a well or by the side of a road. These villages grew in size until one merged into another and we were surrounded by houses. The road was smooth and firm now, metalled with a fine gravel that shone in the sunshine. There was no mistaking the city, as the great spires of Chichester Cathedral loomed before us. It was formed in the abstracted shape of a cat's paw, with four parallel naves joining in the rounded altar space. Each of the four naves was topped by a tall thin glass spire, forming a claw in the sky, with a fine round dome over the altar, topped in coloured glass. I remembered that this modern masterpiece had been a matter of some understandable controversy in the press. Bishop Redfur had defended it, explaining the symbolism behind the design and saying that it was incumbent on the modern clergy to stay in touch with the modern world in every respect. 'We must touch noses with both young and old. The antique is not the only source of the divine.' I wondered guiltily how far this policy had led him to embrace the dancers at the Red Windmill.

The dog cart juddered to a halt and we jumped down onto the ground with gratitude. The hound accepted our tip with a gruff bark, and wriggled out of his harness. He headed straight for the beer-tubs laid out for this purpose at the inn where we had stopped. It reminded me that we had not eaten a morsel since breakfast and, it being nearly noon, I persuaded Toby to stop here for an early lunch. It was largely a dog's inn, but a few things on the menu looked edible, and when pressed the barmaid admitted to a small stock of dried fish. We sat at a small wooden bench outside the inn, watching the carts rolling in and dropping their customers, and listened to a mixture of birdsong, and the ravenous dogs gnawing at their food inside. Some things will destroy even the keenest appetite, and we were soon on our way after picking at our food. We strolled into the town, admiring the classical buildings ranged in neat rows and half-moons about smart, clipped gardens. Close by the cathedral was the most fashionable part of the town. Ladies with bright feathered hats and gentlecats in smart white collars paraded along, nannies following behind them with basketfuls of kittens. We came round a corner and were confronted by the cathedral.

I must admit that despite the Bishop's wise words, I found it rather painful to see. My favourite sort of church is a converted Yooman one, or one built in that ancient style, preferably a little ragged at the corners, with pews worn smooth by a thousand furry coats, and tales from the life of Bast picked out in faded colours on the lime-washed walls. This was far too sleek and spiky for my liking, with the tall glass spires raking the sky, atop the thin arched door in front of us. The Bishop's lodgings were adjacent to the cathedral, being a very comfortable looking manor house, set in a walled garden, just to the east. The graveyard, naturally, lay to the west. However Toby had seen my wince of distaste and persuaded me to take another moment to give the construction a fair chance. We passed inside the door, and I was lost for words.

The whole of the cathedral roof was covered in glass, of many different colours, laid out in gorgeous patterns. Down the centre of the aisle a river of blue glass flowed over our heads, casting a sparkling light like liquid water onto the white marble floor. Over the altar, the light turned green, with a picture of trees and fields set out in glass in a circular ceiling spanning the whole of the central space. It was an astonishing feat of engineering, and astonishingly beautiful. Quite a throng of worshippers sat in the fresh-cut pews, some praying with bent heads, others gazing up at the sunlit wonders above. Perhaps they were praying too. We walked down the aisle in a daze, so it was no surprise that we bumped into the worshipper right in front of the altar, crouched so low that his nose touched the floor.

"Ah, Bishop Redfur," said Toby "We have been looking for you."

11
REDFUR

The Bishop leapt up and spun around. "What the - who are you?" he demanded

"Delighted to meet your Reverence" said Toby. "I am Toby Hunter, detective, and this is my friend and colleague Surgeon Robert Gentlepaw. Might we have a word?"

Bishop Redfur was a tall, elegant cat, of middle age, wearing the simple collar of Bast and two plain gold stud earrings. A rich embroidered stole about his neck hung almost to the ground. His fur matched the heritage of his name, for he was a handsome tawny orange-gold, streaked with white and a colour that was almost red. His eyes were a very pale green. I am no judge of these things, but I believe he was thought to be quite handsome. He appraised us quickly, with a calculating look, and ushered us out of the cathedral, nodding and smiling at his parishioners as he went. Redfur brushed aside a worried looking curate as we entered his residence, but carefully showed his lack of anxiety to any onlooker by pointing out various choice and exotic garden plants to us. He had just finished forcing our admiration of a very fine wisteria, twined about the door, when he ushered us inside to his study, and turned to us with a face like thunder.

"Now what in the name of Cerberus' claws do you mean by bursting in on me in the Palace of Bast in that way? How dare you?" Toby had a gentle smile upon his face and took one of the very comfortable seats which had not been offered. I followed suit.

"I rather think by the manner in which you have received us, your Reverence, that you know very well what our mission is, and what you have to do with it."

"Nonsense! And call me Bishop or Redfur, by the way, half the town seems to do so. This 'Reverence' stuff is all rather old-fashioned, don't you think?" He had instantly and startlingly changed tack, and threw all his not inconsiderable charm at us. Toby was duly unimpressed.

"Well then, Bishop," he said, "Perhaps you will be kind enough to tell me what was the last time you saw Lucinda Lexington?" The Bishop expertly wrestled a scowl into a wry smile.

"You seem to know all about it, detective. Why don't you tell me?" Toby sighed and pulled out his clawbook, turning as I saw, but the Bishop did not, to consult an entirely blank page.

Redfur scowled and barked, "I last saw her in March. A long time ago."

Toby tapped at his notebook, "Truly, Bishop, that does not accord with my records. I think it was a Monday, if that helps, not the Sabbath."

I was pretty sure that Toby's sarcasm did not help at any rate, and I threw the Bishop a small plank to cling to in these choppy waters.

"Mr Hunter and myself have been investigating the tragic death of the young lady, and we have been obliged to speak to any ah, I mean to any known acquaintances of hers, no matter how slight."

Redfur gave us both a slow unhappy look, and appeared to reach a decision. "I suppose there is no avoiding it. Though I cannot understand - I was very careful... well, in any case. I cannot exactly remember the date but I swore never to see her again."

"You parted on good terms?" Toby asked, scribbling a doodle in his pad.

"Yes, indeed - Miss Lexington... Perhaps I had better explain a little?"

"Let me guess, Bishop. You met Lucinda at a social function perhaps?"

"I do not tend to - that is to say - I do not frequent such places as the Red Windmill."

"You know it then?"

"Yes, but, I have only ever visited there out of hours. When there was no show."

"To meet Lucinda?"

"Yes. We became acquainted at - of all things - a charitable ball thrown by Prince Hector. She was there in company with a Member of Parliament, so I believed her to be quite respectable."

"Why should you take acquaintance with an MP to be any guarantee?"

Redfur winced and carried on, "We talked. I found her most engaging - challenging. Not many cats are bold enough to discuss religion in a robust way with a Bishop. The majority of females that I meet want to discuss charitable fetes and christenings with me - not points of philosophy."

"And she was attractive."

"I meet a great many attractive female cats - but for some reason this" he tugged at the collar "renders me neutral so far as most are concerned. She spoke to me in quite a different way, and I liked it."

"So you went to see her."

"Yes - but I soon realised the nature of her employment meant that it would be difficult for me to continue the friendship."

"Despite your precautions?"

"I met her mostly in Worthing! What a worthy place it is, and I flatter myself that I was not recognised there."

I interjected "What? Only a few miles from your own diocese? Surely you could not pass unnoticed."

"Oh you would be surprised" said the Bishop. "My picture is not often in the newspapers. And besides..."

"Besides," Toby finished for him. "I imagine you removed your collar and earrings?"

Redfur looked a little ashamed. "I am not ashamed" he declared, implausibly. "In some ways I would have felt it an honourable and a good thing if I could have drawn her away from her life on the edge of respectability. But..."

"You would have found it difficult to explain to your ladies with their tea and cakes and raffle tickets."

"Quite so. And so I told her in March that we could not meet again. She was quite calm about it."

"March?" I began but Toby hushed me with a pinch to my forepaw.

"She did not make any demands of you?" he asked. "Demands? Certainly not. What could I give her in any case? I am not a rich cat."

From where I sat I could see at least five works of art that any museum would be proud to own. The furniture was well-covered in plush new fabrics, the whole spotlessly clean, and the claws of servants clicked briskly along the corridor outside.

"Perhaps not compared to a Prince." I muttered grimly. Toby, however, was clearly satisfied. He stood up to go, sweeping up his hat, and bowed a nosegreeting to the Bishop.

"We are grateful for your indulgence in meeting us, your Reverence. Perhaps you could clear up just one final point?"

"By all means," said the Bishop, bowing back to us both, and visibly relieved. "Just why, having so carefully extricated yourself from this blackmailer, did you go back to visit her again in May?"

The Bishop gaped at him for a moment, his whiskers bristling with shock and fear. His tail thrashed wildly, knocking over a teacup as he fought to control his temper. A maid rushed to the door and was almost knocked over too as he jumped over and slammed it shut in her face.

"How dare you Sir?" he cried. "Have you not believed a word of my explanation? Do you have no faith?"

"Oh I have every faith in the nature of cats to be quite unchanging. And therefore rarely to be trusted," Toby smiled.

"You had better leave" said Redfur, choked by emotion. "Think on your sins."

"By all means. We'll see ourselves out" said Toby.

12

STEAK AND SUSPICIONS

I insisted on a decent lunch to sustain us before our return to Brighton, and on the advice of a passing gentlecat, whose girth assured me of his solid interest in food, we made our way to the 'Dog's Collar' a few streets away from the Cathedral. A mouthwatering menu was presented to us, alongside a complimentary bowl of fried sprats, and foaming mugs of nip-beer. I spent a happy few moments alternating between the three, before deciding on a steak and eggs. Toby, however, had not touched sprats, menu or beer, and was staring out across the room, looking at nothing, his mind in fierce calculation. He suddenly slammed down a paw on the table, in a move unhappily timed so as to scare off the approaching waitress, and barked at me,

"We have missed some vital point, Robbie. Help me - we must start again."

I hoped sincerely, though not out loud, that this would not necessitate any immediate removal from the spot, as the quality of the sprats encouraged me greatly regarding the impending meal. I cautiously picked up my beer and looked interested.

"I have been blinded by the obvious - vain over solving the trivial puzzle of the numbers in Lucinda's diary. That led us to these four suspects, Royal, Religious, Political and Legal. But who is to say that one of them did it? Do we really have any more clue about the inner life of Lucinda Lexington herself?"

"Er - don't we?" I hoped to encourage this conversation along with minimal intervention, as the nervous waitress had just slid my plate of steak and eggs onto the table, before jumping away from my vehement companion.

"Well - she continues from beyond the grave to live up to my initial estimation. She used these cats to gain status, influence. She found it amusing to toy with their emotions, but she was no real blackmailer. One or two of them seem even to have been truly in love with her. Alleyfeather, and indeed Redfur to some extent. But - I have seen no clear motive from what we have learned why any one of them should be moved to kill. What if the real truth of this lies elsewhere?"

I hastily swallowed a mouthful of egg in time to burble "Where?"

"Somewhere in the Red Windmill. Something has been tapping at my mind since our visit there. We saw something that reminded me... of what I don't know. But I feel sure it was significant. Robbie, you can always help me with your simple take on matters. What or who did we see at the Windmill? From the beginning?"

With regret I put down my fork and cast back my mind to that evening. "Well the Chanteuse, not quite as advertised I think we agreed, but a wonderful singer. Then Dickie the compere, then..."

Toby raised an admonishing paw "You have missed someone out."

"Already?"

"The pianist. The Chanteuse was accompanied by a piano player. You did not notice him?"

"Ah - no, not especially. "

"Well, in that case it does not matter. Still, we must open our minds. "

"Hmph. Then it was the Ribbon Dancers. Very good I thought they were - all those different colours, making the shapes like that. Clever stuff. Then it was ..."

"Wait!" barked Toby, a familiar glitter in his eye. "Ribbons! It was staring us in the face."

"What?"

"There is something else behind all this - Lucinda wore a black ribbon, didn't she. And on our first day in Brighton, did you not notice the preponderance of females on the beach wearing ribbons?"

"Some local fashion I thought."

"But the colours were all different. When ladies declare that pink ribbons are the thing, they will all wear pink ribbons. No - this looked more - tribal. Clannish. We need to find out more about ribbons. Now carry on."

I wondered if my friend were quite well, to go on about such a trivial point when so much was at stake, but I had managed to sneak another mouthful of steak, and a sense of bonhomie was washing over me with my second nip beer.

"Then it was the two comedians - 'Buttons and Bells'. Not very funny I thought."

"The Judge thought they were." "Perhaps they were having a bad night." I soothed diplomatically.

"Buttons and Bells and ribbons." Toby muttered. "Haberdashery!"

"No need to take offence old chap." Toby threw me a warning glance, but chuckled nonetheless. "Perhaps it is nonsense after all, but still I find it significant. Who next?"

"Then Victoria Gingersnap, though of course we did not speak to her at that time. Then the show ended, and we met that appalling old martinet, the Redclaw woman."

"I found her rather impressive."

"You fear neither cat nor ghost. Still I thought she was quite horrible."

"Young Tinker was more to your taste I think"

"She was barely out of school. Besides I fancy Bradley Bell is taking her under his paw."

"I think you are right there." I finished my meal and sat back with a happy sigh. The Collar had lived up to its reputation. Toby finished picking at a sardine and pushed aside the bones.

"There is only one thing left to be done." he declared.

"Robbie, we must go and buy some ribbons!"

13
THE PINK RIBBONS

We got back to Brighton quite late on that day, having taken the more comfortable but slowish route. Toby got me up unconscionably early the next day to trawl the Brighton Laines for haberdasheries. One or two admitted there had been a surge in interest for pink ribbon, but could put no reason to it. We visited some half dozen of these disturbingly female establishments, pawing aimlessly at piles of shining buttons, before something caught Toby's eye. "Pink ribbons!" he hissed in my ear. Two very young and glossy females with sharp pointed ears, long white whiskers and excitable tails were giggling together in a corner, trying various thicknesses of pink ribbon against their throats. They came to a decision and purchased a lace variety. As it was wrapped for them I began to step towards them, but Toby gripped my arm, and bade me be quiet. They left the shop, and we waited a moment, before abandoning our buttons and following. The Brighton Laines are a teeming maze of streets, full of strange little shops selling sundry items that the average cat about town can have no use for whatever. However the lady of his household, should she be on an unending search for the perfect tea towel, exactly the right shade of porcelain egg cup, or a comical birthday card for that troublesome nephew will find her heaven here. And should the gentlecat be of a more discerning nature, and require a seventeenth variety of snuff, or a very particular angle to the cut of his collar, he too can be accommodated by the Laines. Both of them, and their mewing infants, will find ample refreshments in the many cafes and restaurants. But all of this commerce leaves little room for the subtle pursuit of interesting females. We made our way as best we could through the crowds, edging around corners just as our quarry disappeared into a mass of fur. I relied heavily on their scent trail, which was happily strong, if rather too redolent of honeysuckle and sugared plums for my taste. The trail led us to a small dark wooden door, squeezed in between an emporium of antiques and a modish art gallery. There was no sign of a name or door-pull, but the ladies had doubtless disappeared therein. We retired to the cafe opposite and waited patiently, ably assisted by some excellent cream cakes. After about half an hour, the ladies emerged, still laughing, and now wearing their pink ribbons. We waited a few more minutes, and then I got one of the greatest shocks of my life. Another cat backed out of the door, locking it carefully behind him, and scanning up and down the street before stepping out and briskly away. It was Corin Fluffs.

I had last seen this scoundrel on the boat back from Alexandria (see The Mouse of Bones) so I knew that there was some chance of him being in England. But what he could have to do with this business I could not fathom. I gaped at Toby, who was fixed with a look of wry displeasure. We both started up without a word and began to follow our new prey. At the junction the trail of honeysuckle scent tripped off in the opposite direction to that being followed by Fluffs, and we followed him at a very careful distance as he wove out of the Laines, and down towards the sea front. Occasionally he stopped and sniffed the air, looking around him with a curious glance, but seemed unconcerned. Finally he stopped in front of a very large, grand white-plastered hotel, right on the seafront. Its lacy black balconies gleamed in the sunlight, and smart butlercats escorted guests to and from their carriages at the front. He whirled around suddenly, giving us an ironic bow, then strode in.

"He saw us!" I groaned, "We shall never catch him now."

"I do not think he will be going very far today." said Toby slowly.

"It is easy enough to duck out of a side window, or jump from a balcony!" I shouted, turning back and forth to try and see where Fluffs would run to.

"Well he might run away from another hotel, but I think not from this one" said Toby. "You see, Robbie, this is Corin Fluffs' hotel."

He pointed to the brass plate fixed by the door. It stated simply 'Old Grand Hotel. C Fluffs, proprietor'. We entered the hotel lobby. It was quite one of the grandest places I had ever seen. A vast chandelier hung from the ceiling high above our heads, in a double-height lobby ringed by a sweeping staircase. Thick plush carpet swallowed up our paws. Butlercats and porters with shining pink buttons on their gold waistcoats marched respectfully behind sleekly comfortable guests. And a small army of maids - each with a pink ribbon - shone and polished every available surface. The rattle of a cocktail shaker shook me out of my reverie. Lounging insolently against the doorway of the bar was Fluffs.

"Care for a bracer, Toby? Or is it a bit early for you? Don't mind if you bring your pet rabbit, we allow them in the lobby y'know."

He poured a cocktail into a tall glass, setting down the shaker on a butler's tray, and sipped nonchalantly, disappearing into the room.

"You - knew?" I gasped, trembling with a mixture of outrage and shock.

"I knew he had opened a business down here - a legitimate business so far as can be readily discovered. But I suspected he would be up to something else."

"But...! Surely! The Murder! Why did you not come and confront him at once?"

"With what, Robbie?" Toby snarled with a rage long bottled and now released. "That is one of the most dangerous cats it has ever been my misfortune to meet. I know, and you do, that he is already responsible for at least one death, but not so in the eyes of the law. He steers a very careful line, and I do not choose to give him ammunition against me by firing accusations that I stand no chance of proving. He is a liar, a cheat and a scoundrel no doubt. By my reckoning, a murderer already. But he is a very clever cat, and I shall stand little chance of bringing him to justice if I walk into his every trap."

He strode into the bar room, and I followed, shaking with emotion. Fluffs offered me a drink as if the vile insult he had just spewed out had evaporated, and I took it, downing the juice in one, then sitting heavily into a plush velvet chair.

"A fine hotel" remarked Toby. "Yours, I take it?"

"I have some very generous backers," said Fluffs with a nasty grin. "They have been kind enough to encourage me to present myself as the sole proprietor. Such shy, retiring types should hardly be in business! But to what do I owe this pleasure? I understood that the Prince himself had invited you down to the seaside. Surely he has done you the honour of arranging some accommodation?"

"You seem to know a great deal about it" smiled Toby, sipping his cocktail. He is a tremendous actor, for though I knew the terrible rage with which he had entered the room, no one could guess at it who saw him now.

"Spot of bother with a dancer, wasn't it? Often the way with the aristocatcy, I find. Can't see past a shapely leg to the hungry twitching whiskers above! In any case, what do you mean to do about it? I suppose you are awash with suspects, so why come bother me? Just for old times sake?"

"As a matter of fact," Toby drawled, " we were following a clue. We detectives are very fond of such things. They can be - illuminating. Well, no doubt we shall see you again soon. Thank you for the drink."

He set down his glass on the polished table, and strode back out of the room. I followed him in a daze as he moved towards the door, then suddenly darted behind a pillar close to the wall in the thronged lobby. I followed him, then watched as Fluffs shot out of the bar room, and down the front steps, darting his head right and left and openly sniffing the air to seek our trail. He was thwarted by the mass of cats behind him, and shrugging unconcernedly, took up a black cane, and set back out again, pausing only to adjust the peaked cap on the cat at the reception desk.

14

THE LOBBY LADIES

Toby slid out from behind the pillar and settled in a high-backed chair beside an unlit fire. He picked up a newspaper and pretended to read. I settled for the 'Hunting Post' and awaited enlightenment. I had not long to wait, for the chatter of the party registering in the lobby died down as their rooms were allocated, and I began to hear the high pitched, giggling conversation of the young ladies behind me. A stage whisper from Toby, from behind his paper set the scene.

"The same ones we followed from the shop, plus an older cat. Can't see her face. Listen carefully."

"Girls, you are keen to begin I suppose? You have your pink ribbons?"

A fit of giggles answered the lady.

"You may put them on now. Rather fun isn't it - a little whim of Mr Fluffs himself, just as he likes to interview all our new girls personally. For the rest it's a strict uniform. But these you may wish to wear outside the hotel. And so he likes the girls to choose and find their own ribbons. You will start as chambermaids..."

"Oh but we heard...!" The lady interrupted sharply.

"Never mind what you heard. The rates are very generous indeed, that you may have heard reported correctly. But the jobs, let us be very clear, are entirely usual - you will have to do the cleaning, or reception work, or wherever you are posted."

"But what about...?" began the other kit. The lady gave a tired sigh.

"If, after three months, you have proven your worth - and your trustworthiness, there may be other opportunities. And they will be worth waiting for. If not, well we remain in need of pretty kits to clean our rooms, but we have no need of idle paws or flapping mouths in this hotel. Now run along, and report to Miss Grimclaws, she is charge of the chambermaids. Oh and of course, should you find anything amiss in the rooms, you will properly report it to me."

I risked a glance over the top of the Post. One of the girls looked sulkily disappointed, but the other was giving the Lady a pointed, curious look.

"Report it - to Miss Grimclaws, you mean?"

"That would depend on what you found, wouldn't it." said the Lady. She stood up, indicating clearly that the discussion was at an end. I caught sight of her face as she turned. She was a thin, grizzled tabby of late middle age, neatly turned out, with a black cap on her head. An unpleasant smile at odds with cruel green eyes distorted her face. Toby closed up his paper and moved sharply towards the exit, doubling back past the reception desk as he went.

"I wonder - I believe a friend of mine checked in here last week, he said. Could I possibly consult the register?" The clerk gave him a long stare.

"Mr Hunter?" he said "I have a message for you from Mr Fluffs." And he passed over an scrawled note.

"Thank you" said Toby, and he laughed sharply, then passed me the note. It read "Thank you for your custom, come again soon."

Once outside I could not wait to be away from the horrid place, and we strode briskly along the seafront, whipped by a sharp onshore breeze and the beginnings of a sea-fog. I cast Toby an anxious glance, but he had a wry smile about his face. He nodded at me and gripped my shoulder.

"Never fear, old friend. Yes, we have been bested today, but we have learned something of value. The real business of this hotel is pretty clear, and of no surprise to us. The pattern of Fluffs' fur is quite unchanged."

"You mean? What business? What are they up to? I thought that grim tabby female took great care to say nothing we could pick upon."

"Quite so - and yet the matter seemed very clear, do you not think? 'Anything amiss in the rooms' she said."

"Yes, isn't that quite the normal and proper business of a chambermaid?"

"I daresay they often remark it, but it is not quite their job. I should think they would be looking more for anything amiss with the rooms, not necessarily what was in them."

"A subtle distinction."

"Yes - but one that I think at least one of the new recruits was quickly alive to. Not least if she had heard some rumour of the business from a friend. Clearly it is blackmail that is afoot here."

"Exactly what Lucinda was suspected of."

"Yes - yet our evidence suggests she was not a blackmailer - or not in fact, although she may have pretended to do it." I stopped striding along and paused, my paws gripping the pale sea-green railings that edged the beach. I looked back at the gleaming white plaster of Fluffs' hotel. Toby at least had come almost to admire the late Lucinda through this investigation. But I knew his feeling for Fluffs was far from kind.

"Could Lucinda have worked for Fluffs?" Toby had stopped beside me and scuffed crossly at the pavement with his claws. There was a longish silence.

"I don't know. She could have done. I have the feeling he would have amused her. But I think he would have pressed her to go further - to get some real advantage over these noble cats, and to use it for his gain. I cannot think, from all we have learned, that she would have done so."

"Not willingly, perhaps?" I offered.

"Ha. She did not seem afraid. Nor was she easily intimidated, as we know. Well, we need to find out more. But we shall need some help. I need to think." Toby abruptly jumped over the railing and down onto the esplanade below.

Several cheap cafes filled the Arches beneath; we entered one and took a table inside near the window. Our view filled with a boiling white fog, through which only the occasional glimpse of pebbles and shadowy strollers could be seen. Moisture clung to the windows and ran down in streaks, washing away the salty haze. I respected Toby's agitation and waited the invitation to speak. I had just taken a large bite of a sardine scone, when he snapped at me.

"What were the names of those two kits at the country house? The younger Pinkpaw kit and her schoolfriend?"

"What? You surely cannot be thinking of involving them in - this!" Toby waved an impatient paw at me.

"Ach, don't be absurd, Doctor. It is the very innocence of a schoolkit that would help us here. I can make no move without being observed by Fluffs. But you see he has a constant need to recruit to his cause, and he clearly has no conscience about drawing in very young ladies. We could learn something more this way without detection."

"But they are children - you cannot possibly send them into harm's way!"

Toby laughed.

"I am no Hound of Hades! There will be no danger I assure you. I simply need their cover. Besides, it could not be more fortuitous. As I recall, the two are at school here, at the Brighton and Hove Academy for Young Ladies."

15
THE SCHOOL FOR SCANDAL

The School was situated on an otherwise residential road, set back in a fine large villa, of very ancient provenance. Its rather ugly portico was sustained by fat Doric columns, and green framed windows echoed the green shades of the girls' uniforms. A rambling complex of other buildings had grown out of this sturdy central point, each reflecting the architectural style of the day, and forming a patchwork with no coherent theme. We observed so much from peering through the gates, but the hard stares of a horrifying sturdy and gimlet-eyed female who was no doubt a teacher, sent us fast on our way.

"How can we get in?" I muttered. "A school like this will hardly allow us an interview with the girls without some letter of commendation from the parents. Such is not likely to be forthcoming as well you know!"

Toby sniffed the air and checked his pocket-watch. "I think we just have time for a spot of tea, Surgeon."

He pulled me towards a coffeeshop on the corner of the road, and we sat at an outside table. Five minutes later a bell went inside the school and a stream of kits, varied in age from 11 to 18 poured out of the school, bedecked with ribbons, jackets and boaters in a deep, gloaming green. Almost all of them descended immediately on the coffee shop, and Lillia was foremost amongst them.

"I observe that this shop is a purveyor of more forms of confectionary deleterious to the teeth than I had previously been aware existed." Toby growled.

"Come, our quarry may need some assistance." Lillia indeed already had an armful of sweets, and her mouth was filled with a large pink lollipop, whilst her friends were shaking the jars of parma violets and rhubarb creams. I approached warily. But too late, I was addressed by her in a loud scream which would surely have brought the police running if it had not turned rapidly to laughter.

"Oh Bast, girls, what a hoot! It's only my pet detectives!" she trilled. "Are you on the tail of a famous villain again?" I had been prepared for rather more gravity from the girl, even fear in association with the difficult memories of our previous encounter. But the young are notoriously resilient, are they not? Or perhaps she did not care to show her more bruised feelings in front of her friends.

Lillia pulled off her boater, threw her lollipop into a pocket and licked her paws.

"What do you want?" she asked, more quietly.

Toby bobbed a nose-greeting. "What an unexpected pleasure, young lady. Might we take advantage of this chance to offer you some refreshment?"

Lillia sniffed contemptuously. "Nonsense," she spat. "Miss Browntail saw you peering in the gate. She's just finished warning half the school there are some suspicious characters lurking about. I mean I didn't realise it was you two but I see now that it must have been. You'd better just tell me. It's nothing - it's not to do with the family, is it?" A slight tremor in her voice finally betrayed the anxiety I had been expecting, and I felt quite queasy again. We had no right to involve this child in more danger. I gripped Toby's shoulder, and tried to forestall his words with my own.

"Truly it was only an accident of fate we are here. We need not detain you." I said.

But too late, Toby had already shepherded the girl to a table. She waved off her friends. I need not have worried. Toby had a plan.

"It's true, we did come here purposely to find you. I think you may be able to help us with an investigation. You are an intelligent kit..."

"I'm seventeen next month!"

"I apologise, an intelligent young lady, so I will tell you the truth, if you can promise me you will not share it with the friends who are doubtless waiting for you in that side alley?"

She paused, gave Toby a hard look in the eyes, and nodded. "Have you by any chance read in the newspapers of the death of a young actress and dancer in Brighton?"

"Lucinda Lexington. I actually saw her dance once."

I gasped. "Surely not at the..."

"The Red Windmill, yes. Some of the girls thought it would be rather a lark. One of them has an elder brother who went there sometimes, and he got us in. Just to see Lucinda. That Redclaw molly who runs the place is hard as nails but she let us have a table for half an hour, as we were already there. Gave us ices too! But then she told Charlotte's brother not to bring us again. And banned him for a month!"

"What a very sensible cat" Toby muttered.

"She was such a wonderful dancer. I'm going to be a dancer one day" she said firmly, with the habit of one who is often told otherwise.

"It is Lucinda's death we are investigating. And we want your help."

"I'm no fool, but I'm no detective, Mr Hunter. What do you want me to do?"

Toby grinned broadly. "For a start I want your hat!"

"What?" Lillia gaped at him open-mouthed, then giggled. "It won't suit you. It doesn't suit me, come to that. I don't mind losing it again if that's all you need. But whatever for?"

"I need to infiltrate a hotel where the staff being taken on are all rather young kits, and I need a good disguise."

Lillia was quite suffused with giggles.

"Well I can tell you that not even a set of false whiskers would fool anyone that you're a schoolkit! Nor your lovely friend the doctor, I'm afraid. There is one girl I think you might ask but not even her blazer would fit you."

"Ah, but it's not for me" said Toby "

Oh! Do you want me to do it? Is it Fluffs' hotel? One of the sixth-form girls did go down there last month, just for a dare and to get the pink ribbon, but she never even saw him."

I could not bear it. "You cannot do anything of the kind. It would be far too dangerous!" I declared.

"Quite right, Robbie" said Toby with an affectionate glance.

"No, we only want to borrow a few items of your uniform for a day - and perhaps yourself for a few moments to add verisimilitude. An actress friend of mine would make the actual approach."

"Oh no!" I cried, "Not..."

"Hush, Robbie! Our friend here is safer the less she knows about it. Now will you help?"

Lillia pulled the lollipop out of her pocket and twirled it thoughtfully before sticking it firmly to the table.

"Can I tell my friends about it afterwards?"

"Yes, by all means, but only when we have found out what we want to know. Before then you would endanger my friend."

She nodded assent. "I shall be in touch shortly" said Toby, and we left Lillia running around the corner to amuse her friends.

"You don't need to tell me where we're going next" I groaned, "Or rather you do, but not why - we're going to meet Gertie and Vera, aren't we."

"Indeed so, my old friend, but aren't you pleased that I am not after all a menace to schoolkits?"

16

BRIGHTON BELLES

Gertie and Vera made a very striking picture of elegant femininity as they strolled along the seafront. Gertie wore a flat straw bonnet, tied under her chin with a broad lilac ribbon. Vera twirled a pale pink parasol to shade her face from the sun. She stopped and laughed as a cat at the edge of the water dipped in a toe, before leaping high in the air in shock at the cold. I observed for a moment this charming and disarming scene, whilst struggling to reconcile it with the true nature of the ladies before me. As I paused in inner turmoil, Vera turned away and saw me. She did not hesitate to laugh. Toby gave my shoulder a sympathetic pat and ran up to meet them. He has always had a great affection for Gertie, ever since he relieved her of a very large diamond she once stole (see The Feline Detective). Gertie Fluff, also known as an acclaimed London actress, had a range of aliases that she donned as easily as a hat. Vera, her beautiful and terrifying niece was in training with her. To what end I had not dared to ask.

"My dear ladies" said Toby "How very good of you to come."

"I would not miss one of your wonderful adventures for the world!" declared Gertie. "Nor would I leave you alone to deal with that vile creature Fluffs."

"Besides, we were getting bored in Paris, weren't we Auntie G?" said Vera, with a coquettish flick of her tail.

"Now then Vera, these gentlemen don't want to hear about our holidays, they have work for us to do."

Toby waved a dismissive paw. "Yes I believe I read about some little mishap in Paris, that emerald coronet. Perhaps it will turn up? These things often do. But you are correct, I have an interesting role for you. At least, I fear primarily for Vera on this occasion. I need you to impersonate a schoolkit. We need to infiltrate Fluffs' hotel, and find out how their blackmailing scam works."

"Blackmail?" sniffed Gertie " I thought you were after a murderer?"

"That I am" said Toby, "But I think Fluffs is somehow connected with both."

"Somehow? You don't seem very certain."

"I am in a little difficulty" Toby admitted.

"We are in something of a tangle but I do need to be sure if Fluffs is involved or not. I know he is up to something, but I don't know if it went so far as murder. I think that Lucinda might have worked for him, or he may have asked her to do so. But I have no proof of anything."

Gertie gave him a penetrating look. "It's a hot day" she declared. "Shall we get an iced cream?"

This suggestion at least met with universal approval, and it was not long before we were all happily seated around the bandstand, tubs of ice cream in our paws. Gertie laid a kindly paw on Toby's arm.

"This confusion is unlike you," she said. "Tell me what you do know. Begin with what first brought you to Brighton."

Toby showed a little embarrassment. "I cannot quite tell you that. A distinguished client, shall we say, had some concerns about Miss Lexington. He feared some exposure which would have put at risk his own marriage plans."

Vera giggled. "Hector you mean? I can't believe Alexandrina is going to marry that fat oaf. Though we are hopeful of an invitation, aren't we Duchess?"

Gertie hissed at her. "Do be quiet, girl and if we do go to that wedding, it shall be as the

Grand Duchess Tatiana and her maid, so don't get airs. Do go on, Toby."

Toby gave her a weary look and continued our tale. "Lucinda was not a blackmailer - or at least this was not her intention in this case. But she was then killed, and we found some notes in her apartment which suggested connections to a number of prominent cats who might have had something to gain by ensuring her silence."

"Who were they?"

"Well beside the Prince, as you seem to know all about it, a Bishop, a Judge and an MP."

Vera whistled, cutting this off abruptly in response to a sharp glance from her aunt. Gertie slowly tapped the claws of her right forepaw on the deckchair.

"The Prince is Hector, the Bishop must be Redfur, the only one I know of with enough fun and as little sense to get entangled, the Judge could be any of them, I'd be surprised if it was only one, but the MP... I don't know. Why do you not think it's one of them then?"

Toby shrugged. "It still could be. Hector I think not, he is not fool enough to ask me to investigate and then have her killed, and not clever enough to do it as a double bluff."

"But the others?"

"Alleyfeather was in love with her!" I declared.

"Discretion, Robbie!" warned Toby. "A little quieter at least, please."

"Alleyfeather, eh?" asked Gertie with a wry smile. "Well I can certainly see why he would not want it known, with the career he has begun to build."

"It was not him" I barked.

"Maybe not, Robbie," Gertie soothed, "but you have two other good suspects there at least. Or could you rule them out in some way?"

"They might claim to have an alibi. I think half of the Bishop's congregation would lie for him, but it matters not when I have no positive proof that either was even there. However I am still missing a firm motive. All of them seemed really to like Lucinda."

"She was very charming" said Gertie.

"You knew her?" I asked

"It's a small world" Gertie smiled. "Yes, I even went to see her show once. I take it you have no suspects at the Red Windmill?"

"Victoria Gingersnap was not sorry she was gone. Indeed she was glad of the opportunity to take her place. But I had no sense she could have been driven to murder."

"Had Lucinda any friends amongst the other performers?"

"She had befriended one of the Ribbon dancers, and the two comic turns seemed kindly disposed towards her. But they were not too helpful to us."

"Actors and Actresses - you will never get straight talking from them" chuckled Gertie.

"They will be playing some part or other decided upon before you ever arrived. Why not let me sniff around the Windmill while Vera plays the schoolkit?"

17

TILTING AT THE WINDMILL

There follows an extract from the Journal of Gertrude Fluff

I was glad to see my old friend Toby Hunter again yesterday; he pulls at my heart strings in a way that no other cat ever has. I think he knows it, but although he has ever been kindly to me, we have never spoken of love. The obstacle between us remains my way of life, which conflicts somewhat with his own rather sober approach. So I assume at any rate, though he is surprisingly lenient when he catches me at some little game. His telegraph had caught me not quite by surprise, as I had expected some trouble to come from the direction of Brighton ever since I saw that the Old Grand Hotel had gone into the gentle care of that reprobate Corin Fluffs. Toby seems to hate him with a passion. I don't care for him myself, scrawny nasty cat that he is, but I think he is careful to steer just the right side of the law, or to keep himself insulated from his crimes. I doubt my friend will ever manage to snare him. Still I am very glad to help Toby in this particular case, for it concerns an old friend of mine. Though I have not mentioned it - no doubt he knows anyway - I knew Lucinda Lexington of old, when she had first pawed the London stage, and did a little of everything. Lucy Locket she was then, and a fine actress she would have made, only that she was a better dancer. We were friends then, the better that she decided to dance for a living, for that left the stage to me. Of course since then I have found a rather better living to be had in relieving foolish and over-rich gentlecats of their family heirlooms, and playing out my roles in the world at large. Still, we had something in common, and I was very sad to hear of her passing. Though we had lost touch recently, she had written to me a few times after we first parted ways. Indeed her last letter had come to tell me of the great opportunity she had found at the Red Windmill. I recall her description of the awful molly that ran the place.

"Quite a witch, but fair, I think. And she recognises a real talent. Some nice folk here, I believe we shall rub along well."

So it was Miss Redclaw that I begged to see first on arrival. She bade me to sit, and barked at some hapless maid to fetch tea, then rudely continued to study some papers, leaving me in contemplative silence while we waited. Having observed Toby at his work for many years, I know better than to speak first, and waited her out with every appearance of calm.

She looked up in the end, snarling at the anxiously waiting maid to go, then demanded, "What do you want?"

"I was a friend of Miss Lexington's - I was most shocked at the manner of her passing, and I wished to pay my respects."

Redclaw stared hard at me, from my hat to my claws. I had worn no particular disguise but I had given perhaps a slight impression of nobility in the quality of my lace trimmings, and the angle at which my bonnet tilted away from my face.

Redclaw waved a grizzled paw at me. "If you were a true friend of Lucinda's you would know her real name."

I smiled, and coarsened my accent. "Lucy, of course, but I wasn't sure that you knew it."

She gave a sharp laugh, choked off with a fit of coughing, then rummaged for some sweets in a drawer.

"I used to smoke the nip-baccy" she said. "Gave it up three years ago on doctor's advice but I'm stuck with the cough. It will do for me in the end."

She put a boiled sweet in her mouth and sucked and crunched on it noisily. "So you did know Lucy. Well, I liked her. She thought me a mean old harridan, but we got along. She worked hard, I paid her regular. We had the measure of each other. Do you know this detective that's investigating?" I considered briefly the risks of denial, but Redclaw seemed too wily by half.

"I do indeed, Miss Redclaw. He's by way of being a friend of mine."

"Such a *lot* of friends you have!"

"Quite so. But I rather thought he might not have heard all you had to tell. We ladies must stick together mustn't we."

"I told him a great deal."

"About Lucinda's hobby, indeed, but not about her life here. You two got along well, was she friendly with all the rest of the cast?"

Redclaw spat out some impurity in her sweet and considered her words. "There can be jealousy. No doubt about that. There was a little trouble there. But I put a stop to it right enough."

"Trouble?"

"A silly prank. Young Gingersnap fancied a turn at the lead, and put itching powder in Lucinda's face cream. She couldn't go on that night and nor could she meet one of her admirers. She was annoyed. Gingersnap had to perform, but I set her straight that this was no way to go on. Docked her pay too."

"And now Victoria has the lead role that she wanted."

"Aye. She's not a patch on my Lucy though. She won't keep it for long, so soon as I can find a decent replacement. Then she'll be back to understudy again."

"She won't be happy with that," I said.

"But it seems like a long leap from itching powder to strangulation."

"Too great a leap for Victoria, on or off the stage."

"What about Corin Fluffs?" The name fell into our conversation like a stone. Redclaw, who had visibly warmed to me, clammed up again.

"We have nothing to do with him here."

"Why shouldn't you? He owns the best hotel in Brighton. Surely some connection would profit you?"

She considered. "Perhaps it would - but I don't know that I like his manner of doing business."

"Oh? And what manner is that?"

She licked her claws, leaving them unsheathed and gleaming on the desk.

"I fancy his guests can find their stay in Brighton more expensive than they expected."

"It's an expensive hotel."

"And no doubt they can afford it. All the best people stay there. And you are right, often they will come for entertainment to the Windmill. Perhaps that is why Fluffs had the idea too."

"Of a connection?"

Redclaw dug her claws into the desk. It was the first real sign of agitation I had seen in her. She did not seem conscious of it, but curled delicate strips of wood away as she pulled them back towards her.

"Can I trust you?" she asked suddenly. "For all I know you work for Fluffs yourself. What are your credentials?"

I racked my brain for some way to reassure her. She was right to be cautious - no doubt she had survived this long in business only through rank cunning. Sentiment for her lost dancer had got me this far, but I had not fully gained her confidence. Then a chance phrase from Lucinda's last letter came back to me.

"Lucy told me that you were sometimes almost motherly to her. Help me to help her."

"She's beyond helping now."

But I spied the moisture in her eye that would have led to a tear in another cat.

"Very well" she said at last. "I hope I shall not regret it. Yes, Fluffs came here - he made a proposition to Lucinda. He was aware that she was a great draw for many of his rich and famous customers, and that they confided in her. He wanted to pay her for information - and then make them pay to keep it quiet."

"Blackmail" I breathed.

"He's a cunning beast. And persistent. She told him straight enough that she would not do it. Lucy enjoyed making her fellows dance, she liked to have influence in the world, but she had no stomach for real blackmail. But he kept coming back. In the end she came to me and I had to tell him to keep away. But he gave me the shivers, and few do."

"So she never worked for him."

"No, just for me, my dear. And for me she danced and sang. Very beautifully she did it, but that was all. The rest was just for her own fun."

"Thank you, Miss Redclaw. Is there anything else that you can tell me that might help?"

"She loved to laugh," and now the tears fell down freely from her eyes.

"My Lucy loved to laugh."

18

AT THE GRAND HOTEL

Vera had befriended young Lillia with little difficulty. Indeed the schoolkit was amused and amazed at the East End cat in equal measure. She was also excited at the possibility of showing off this exotic creature to her school friends when the adventure was done. So while Gertie had taken herself off to the Red Windmill, we set about the infiltration of Fluffs' lair at the Grand Hotel. Lillia's uniform fitted Vera very well - at least she wore only the straw boater and pelisse, which fitted her head and shoulders convincingly. Then Vera, flanked by Lillia and her friend Noemi took a stroll along the seafront with such fits of giggles as made every passer by stare. Fortunately this could only add to the verisimilitude of our little fiction, of a sixth-form schoolkit taking a maid's job for the summer holidays. Vera bade her school friends a loud goodbye in the lobby of the hotel, and they skipped away round the corner. She boldly rang the reception bell, and I slipped into the reading chair behind a pillar to listen in. Toby had sanctioned this move, both to afford Vera some protection if necessary (she had scorned this motive) and by way of a diversion for Fluffs himself if he were about.

Toby opined that "He will be annoyed rather than alarmed by your presence, Robbie - he will imagine that I have sent you to keep watch in some way, and not that you are protecting some unknown third agent. I think we may risk it."

Vera had rigged her disguise very carefully. In addition to the hat and cape, she wore dark powder and streaks of dye to alter her natural colouring, and dark-rimmed glasses, subtly tinted to change the hue of her eyes. Her slim figure could not be easily disguised, but remained convincing as that of a younger cat. She tapped her claws in a little ditty on the countertop, in what I hoped was a pretence at nervousness.

"May I help you, Miss?" asked the reception desk cat. He was a very tall and sleek grey-furred cat, with muddy green eyes and a small white patch under his chin. A label on his hat declared him to be 'Benson'.

"Yes please, Benson" giggled Vera, "I want a pink ribbon!"

"The Brighton Laines are full of haberdashers, Miss. Perhaps you had best look there. This is a hotel."

He turned aside and began to rummage amongst the room keys. Vera gave a very convincing impression of a spoilt and thwarted teenager.

"Don't be mean! I want one! The other girls told me this is the place to come. I can work just as well as anyone. What do I have to do?"

On this last point she lowered her voice and laid her neat little paw onto Benson's own.

He sighed and lowered his voice. "Miss, there may be a position open but the very first thing you must do is to be more discreet. There are customers in the lobby and they expect the staff here to be seen and not heard. Or not even seen. If you are quite certain I shall call Miss Cache"

"Do I not even meet Mr Fluffs then?"

"You can meet him in due course if you are accepted. He is a very busy cat." Benson pressed a small button under the counter. "Wait over there" he asked, with a kindly smile.

Vera stalked past me with no sign of recognition, and sat down in one of the chairs near the door with a loud sigh. After a short interval, the same thin tabby cat with a pinched face that we had seen before emerged from a dark side door. She studied Vera from a distance before stalking over and sitting down. She nodded in hint of a nosegreeting, and gestured for Vera to begin.

"My name is Violet Greenclaws" said Vera, "I was told there was interesting work to be had here."

"If cleaning rooms interests you, young lady? I suggest your parents might be rather disappointed if that were the use you wanted to make of your education?"

Vera tutted and pulled off her boater. "Oh this" she said carelessly, tossing it onto the floor. "Well of course not, but I wanted to make a bit of money over the holidays. My allowance doesn't go very far, and I'm a boarder, so my parents needn't know."

The lady's whiskers twitched with amusement. "I suppose you can read, do arithmetic?"

"Of course! What a question!"

"Have you learned any foreign languages? French, German, Italian?"

"I have a little French. I'm studying Italian as my extra subject this term. Do you have much call for Italian-speaking chambermaids?"

"We have guests from all over the world. It is pleasant to be able to offer our guests some assistance in their own language. You are an inquisitive soul."

"I take an interest in my surroundings."

"Such as?"

"Such as - who am I talking to?"

"You may address me as Miss Caché"

"Catchit?"

"Caché. Now then, despite your casual manner, you are fortunate in your timing. We happen to have some vacancies and some important guests about to arrive. Can you start immediately?"

"Oh!" None of us had expected this.

"Well, yes, I suppose so. I have some lessons this afternoon but my friends might cover for me."

"Send them a message then. I believe they are still waiting for you outside the hotel. Then come back at once. I have a uniform for you and you can go straight up and begin work."

Either this was a great and lucky chance or our plan had somehow been detected and Vera was already in great danger. There seemed no way to know which. Vera simply nodded and exited the door of the hotel to usher Lillia and Noemi away. She returned without looking at me, and Caché followed her into the lift. I was unsure what to do, and watched the lift go up to the top floor in an agony of suspense. I waited a good hour, but Vera had not returned, and I could drink no more coffee. No word of the newspapers I perused could I recall. I had been sent only to observe, but this too now seemed futile. I had almost decided to leave and report back on progress, when I saw Corin Fluffs himself enter the lobby.

He wore a glossy top hat, tilted rakishly to one side, and a neat black bow tie on top of his dusty grey fur. He strode boldly in, and paused right on the central spot of the plush carpet, tilting his angular head right and left and breathing deeply, scenting and seeing all in his kingdom. He had not seemed even to flicker in this survey, but turned on the spot and stalked directly towards me.

"Why it's Toby Hunter's pet rabbit!" he hissed. "I shouldn't have thought to see you here again. Have you fallen quite in love with my little hotel already? Or can you simply not keep away from our sardines?"

The cat had a nasty ability to torment me with his every word, yet for Vera's sake I tried not to react.

"I was just leaving," I mumbled, knocking over my coffee cup in my agitation to get up quickly.

"Indeed you are, Surgeon, and I'll thank you to tell your Master not to sully my lobby with your presence again. If he wants to keep an eye on me he can do me the small courtesy of coming himself."

He stopped and observed the spreading coffee stain on the floor, but before he could speak a nervous looking Benson was already scrubbing at it. I stumbled out of the lobby, half blinded by the brightness of the sunlight outside, and headed to the rendezvous point with Toby. I had failed him.

19
A MERRY TROUPE OF PLAYERS

Extract from the journal of Gertrude Fluff

Before leaving the Windmill I thought I had better see if any further insight could be gained from bringing a female touch to the interrogation of the actors and players themselves. I found them downstairs at rehearsals, and watched for a while from a corner seat, before a heavy breath on my neck told me I was not alone.

"We don't usually allow anyone in to the rehearsals, Miss...?"

I recognised him at once from Toby's description - "Black greying fur, badly dyed in spots, whiskers plaited in a ridiculous style, eyes like a goldfish" - it was Dicky Bowpaws who addressed me.

"So I understand" I said coolly, and resumed my observation. He was undeterred.

"You a friend of Miss Redclaw?" he asked, somehow inserting into that question complete incredulity that she might have a friend.

"A friend of Lucinda's" I said.

He sat next to me and we contemplated the divine music of La Chanteuse. She sang of love and loss, and the room fell silent. Then, in odd juxtaposition, it was the comic act, Buttons and Bells. They were quite dreadful! Something was badly amiss with their timing, and they could barely raise a smile at their own poor jokes. Only 'Bells' managed a hearty laugh when 'Buttons' tripped over a long ribbon left on the stage and fell on his own tail. Dicky stopped them after a few minutes and spoke to them quietly on the stage before returning. The routine picked up a little, but they finished shortly after.

"They are usually pretty funny, but they've been all to pieces since Lucinda died" he sighed. I have noticed that people will often talk to a stranger far more freely than anyone else, especially if one seems quite uninterested. Perhaps it is some unconscious echo of a confessional box, hearing and absorbing your inner thoughts without much reaction, not even the requirement of a penance. I merely blinked to let him know I was listening, and he rambled on.

"Richard was fairly sweet on her, I reckon. They were thick as thieves some days, anyhow. And he looked out for her when the fans came knocking. Anyway," he sighed "She won't be back now. And this one isn't much use."

He waved an unhappy paw at Victoria Gingersnap, now turning cartwheels across the stage. "No sense of style, no dignity to it. First she said she'd keep the act the same, but now she thinks it's dull. Wanted it more modern. Well I could have told her it was no good, in fact I did tell her. But will she listen?"

His questions, as the rest of his rambling, required no answer. But Dicky broke off his own reverie and went up to remonstrate with Victoria. As each act finished they left the stage, and went backstage for some refreshment, before reappearing to sit politely in front of each others' acts. La Chanteuse had sat at a table in front of us, Victoria went off, and the comics were still gone as the Ribbon Dancers appeared and began to rush about the stage, forming frenzied patterns in the air with their coloured trails. It was just as I thought I saw a cat's face hover in the air, sparkling in green and blue amidst their twirling paws that I heard a long and terrible scream. The ribbon sticks clattered to the floor and Dicky jumped up in alarm.

"What in Bast's name was that?" he shouted and ran towards the curtains. Some hidden paw pulled the rope to draw them back, and the Ribbon Dancers shuffled aside to reveal a screaming Victoria, holding bloodied paws aloft. She stood beside the body of Richard 'Buttons' Greywhiskers, who was never to joke again.

We all froze for a moment, before I leapt up and ran to the exit. I heard paws scrabbling up the stairs ahead of me, but I had waited an instant too long, and by the time I reached the front door, he, or she had disappeared. I screamed for help, and a policecat was summoned. In the meantime I went back down into the Red Windmill, and the horror that waited on the stage.

I could barely believe the sight in front of me. It did look like a scene from a play; the corpse sprawled across the centre of the stage, blood seeping in a wide pool around it. A weeping and incoherent Victoria Gingersnap was curled up to one side, as Dicky made useless efforts to comfort her. A gaggle of Ribbon Dancers twittered about in front, clinging to one another for reassurance. Bradley Bellringer was sat upright to the side of his partner's corpse, apparently rigid with shock, his mouth opening and closing fishlike, without a sound. The absurd theatricality of the scene was completed as a slow, classical tune began on the piano behind me. La Chanteuse for some reason had begun to play, but as I watched her paws slowly move, tears fell down onto the keys. Clearly, a strong dose of sense and practicality was required.

I took a grip of the nearest cluster of Ribbon Dancers, and ordered them to go and make strong sweet tea for everyone. They responded well to activity, and soon even the policecat, now ushering the players still able to move from the stage, was equipped with a cup. I pulled Victoria away from Dicky and gave her a hard pinch, which stemmed her tears. As I suspected, she was more in shock and crying for herself than genuinely upset, and was soon persuaded to take herself off to her dressing room. Bradley I was more concerned about. He seemed unable to speak, but one of the Dancers, Tinker, took a special interest in him, to which he responded somewhat. I left him in her care. Dicky seemed rather at a loss and I gave him the unwelcome task of advising his employer of the latest loss to her troupe of performers. This left me free to follow Victoria to her room where I pounced on the opportunity to discover and test her story while she sniffed and dabbed at her eyes. It had not escaped my attention that this murder had been a desperate and surely unplanned act. It had occurred almost under the noses of a roomful of witnesses, and Victoria, if not the perpetrator herself, must surely have seen him.

"What happened?" I asked, gently.

"I don't know, I don't know." she replied, dazedly.

"You must think, child. Don't you realise that this puts you in danger too?"

"You mean? He meant to kill me?"

I had not meant any such thing, but it gave me pause for thought. What was the motive for this latest killing? It had to be connected with Lucinda's death, a mere coincidence of this magnitude was inconceivable. And yet - it made no sense. If the issue was blackmail, real or imagined, then surely the threat had died with the blackmailer. If Corin Fluffs had been taking revenge for Lucinda's refusal to fit in with his plans, then why come back after another of the Red Windmill players? Beyond the fact that they worked together, what was the connection between Buttons and Lucinda? Unless Victoria was right and she was the intended victim? Could some religious mania be at play here, seeking out female cats whose behaviour it found intolerable? Surely a nonsense in this modern age and yet...?

I asked again, less softly. "Tell me what happened."

Victoria spoke in an airy voice, as if she were floating lightly above the room, viewing her own memories with the necessary detachment.

"I had just finished my act, and I went backstage to wash my face. Buttons was coming out of his dressing room. I think he'd been putting ointment on his tail, I could smell the herbs and oil. Then this figure appeared from nowhere, he had a black cloak on and a mask and I couldn't see his face. He came towards me, but Buttons grabbed him and they fought, then I smelled metal and blood. Buttons fell down, and I couldn't understand it, he wouldn't move, his eyes closed..."

"Did he say anything?"

"He said, 'Lucinda' ".

20
RENDEZVOUS

Our meeting point with Toby was the cafe in the gardens just to the side of the Sandcastle. By Royal decree these have been declared to be a public space, and are a rather mixed blessing to the town council, who maintain them for public use. One of the ways in which they recoup the cost is the cafe, which provides excellent fare at a very reasonable price. However I was in no condition to enjoy any part of the fine spread which Toby had caused to be set out for our gathering. I was first to arrive, and was directed by the waitress to the table which had been reserved for us. Toby arrived shortly after me, and noted with alarm that the salmon sandwiches, chilled creams, mint salad and fried sardines were quite untouched.

"My dear fellow," he asked, gripping my shoulder, "Are you unwell?"

"Sick at heart," I replied. "I am most concerned about Vera, they asked her to begin right away and some unpleasant female with a French sounding name took her off upstairs. I waited for nearly an hour before I came to find you. Where have you been?"

Toby looked at me thoughtfully and sat down, then poured the tea. "Have a sardine at least, Robbie, they look awfully good. Don't be concerned about Vera. She is not a kitten, after all, and is well aware of our views on Fluffs. Even he would not I think commit a cold blooded murder without reason. If he suspected her, he would simply send her away. He will not get blood on his paws - especially in his own hotel - if he can help it. She is probably more safe there than anywhere right now. I am rather more bothered as to where Gertie has got to. A simple jaunt to Rottingdean should not have taken this long, unless the dog cart has broken an axle."

I recognised the sense of his words, and took a bite of sardine. It had a reassuring crunch, and sweetly salty tang of the sea. While my mouth was full, Toby began to explain his own wanderings, but we were interrupted by Gertie's arrival, which threw us into confusion. She sat down abruptly and seized a sandwich as if her life depended on it.

Munching angrily between words, she spluttered out, first, "Buttons is dead!", and then "Where's Vera?"

The next half an hour was a flurry of explanations, as first Gertie, then I told our stories, and Toby chivvied us along to add a detail here or there, or to skate over (on my part only I admit) overly florid excursions into description. We paused over a pot of tea and our cream pots to think for a moment. Then I recalled that I had never had an answer to my first question, just as Gertie asked it for me.

"But what have you been doing Toby?"

"I went for a walk" he said. "I needed to think. And now I need to think again. I had begun to imagine that I saw a chink of sense, that this was finally the way in which we could pin down that villain Fluffs. But now, I can make no sense of it at all. Gertie, tell me again who was not in your sight between the moment Buttons disappeared behind the curtain and when the body was found?"

"I could see Dicky, he was talking to me, the Ribbon Dancers were on stage, Bells and La Chanteuse had already come back out."

"So only Victoria was out of sight."

"Yes, but someone attacked her - or Buttons anyway, and I did hear footsteps running away."

"Are you certain? It was a terrifying moment. Could you have been carried away by the dramatic scene set for you?" Gertie is quite the master of a withering glance. I only caught the edge of this one as it was directed at Toby.

"No, very well then, you heard someone else running up the stairs. But that need not have been the assailant. It could have been Victoria."

I interrupted, "You have forgotten two other cats." They both stared at me as if the teapot had spoken.

"Miss Redclaw, and Mittens, her maid" I said, sulkily. "I know it's unlikely, but you always say, Toby..."

"That the unlikely trumps the impossible every day. You are quite right to remind me of it, Robbie. Though I count Mittens capable of no greater crime than putting the wrong sort of milk in her mistress' tea."

"Redclaw did not kill Lucinda!" Gertie exclaimed loudly.

"Could she have killed Buttons?" asked Toby .

She hesitated. "Perhaps, possibly, if she thought he had been the one to kill Lucinda."

"Two killers?" I pondered, "One crime flowing from the other, but not both directly from the same cause?"

"Yes, that's possible" said Toby. "But still we have no clear motive for the first crime. This should make things simpler, but it seems to complicate matters. Can we at least eliminate Corin Fluffs?"

"Do you want to?" I asked.

"I'd like to feel I had some better idea today who killed Lucinda than I did yesterday, considering another cat has died and I have done nothing to prevent it."

"Fluffs was at The Grand at about half past three. What time was Buttons killed?" I asked.

"About three. So he could have been there, and just made it back to the Grand to see you" said Gertie.

"In a greyhound cab? Perhaps. It doesn't matter - if Fluffs had wanted Buttons dead, he could have had it done by a hired paw, and we should be none the wiser. If he needs an alibi, he will have one no doubt. Are you certain it was a cat you heard on the stairs? Could it even have been a dog?"

"Perhaps a very small one, but even if my ears deceived me, I am sure it was the scent of a cat. A male cat."

"This helps not at all." Toby nibbled at his claws and I licked a few crumbs from the sardine plate, which was unaccountably empty.

A gloomy silence fell. I looked at the clock on the wall, which was ticking past five. "It's getting late" I said.

"Yes, it looks like Vera will not meet us this afternoon. Perhaps we had better leave a message for her. I'll ask Lillia to drop a note for her into the hotel lobby, with further instructions."

"And then?"

"Let us pray to the God's ears and whiskers that Vera is safe and has some clue for us. Without it we are sunk!"

21
A CHAMBERMAID'S TALE

We paced, tails low and twitching, along the Brighton Pier just after seven at night, watching the sun sliding ever lower in the sky. Finally, with enormous relief, I observed Vera skittering towards us and we retired to a quiet corner of the public bar at the very far end of the pier to hear her tale.

"I could not get away before!" she declared with obvious excitement. "They had several distinguished guests arriving today, some girls they had taken on yesterday had gone and they truly needed the extra paws. I have been brushing carpets and scrubbing floors!" She laughed, then paused seeing our grim faces. "What's wrong? I could not send you any word, you know that."

"Buttons, the comic at the Windmill, is dead," said Gertie. "It happened while I was there. He was stabbed."

"Oh!" Vera squealed, then clung to her Auntie like a kitten. "Oh! Were you in danger, did you see who did it?"

"No, and unfortunately, no," said Gertie. "But it adds to our urgent need to find who is running riot here. What can you tell us?"

Toby leaned over and touched her paw lightly with his own. "Tell us everything, Vera, we don't know what may be important."

She sipped slowly at her nipjuice and began. "Well you saw that Caché female that took me away? We went straight up to the top floor in the lift, where she made me put on some uniform from a little store cupboard. Just a white cap, and a pink ribbon she took from a drawer. I left the school things there. Then she marched me to meet an even worse old tabby called Grimclaws. There were a dozen maids running about trying to get the rooms ready. There are four special suites on the top floor for VIP visitors, three are occupied already - though I shall tell you something about that in a moment - but one had to be made ready for someone coming today. And such a fuss they made about it! The room must be spotless, every wall and corner, the divans shining white and ironed flat as a board. Not a stray hair must be anywhere. Then flowers on every surface. It was like cleaning a house; there's a bedroom, sitting room, washroom, and a closet for clothes bigger than my bedroom!

Then three more guests were arriving today on other floors. One very grand room on the floor below, and two other new guests to come in ordinary rooms. That's on top of all the normal cleaning."

"And did you observe anything other than 'normal cleaning'?" said Toby.

"Oh yes. But let me keep the tale in order or I shall lose my way. First Grimclaws took a look at me and turned over my paws. She gave me a funny look but said I'd do. She sent me downstairs to clean the grand room. Just gave me a mop and bucket and a dustpan and brush, and off I went! Well I was at that for an hour, for she drilled into me first just how thorough to be. Just as well, for as I was sweeping up the last dustings she flung open the door to inspect my work. She said nothing, but was pleased I think, for then she crooked a claw at me and led me along the corridor to another of the little service cupboards they have on every floor. Then she gave me instructions for cleaning another of the rooms, one that was still occupied."

"By who?"

"Oh, some businesscat here doing something at the bank."

"Rather an expensive room for a banking clerk, wasn't it?" I asked.

"You would think so, wouldn't you. Apparently the hotel has been offering a series of 'commercial discounts' to various carefully selected businesses, banks, legal firms, even government offices, so it is almost always full. It's by far the best hotel any of these cats can get in Brighton at the price. Some of the most prestigious customers get the rooms for free, or at half the advertised price. Or else they are moved to a better room than paid for on arrival."

"How do they explain that?" asked Toby

"They say it's a sort of advertisement, getting the hotel going again under its new management. I can tell you it keeps the chambermaids busy anyway. At the end of my cleaning instructions Grimclaws said there was just one more thing to know. 'Be as thorough as you like,' she said, 'you never know what dirt has fallen into a briefcase, or a drawer, or a washbag. This is a very clean hotel. So you bring any such dirt that you find to me. I can clean it up.' And she gave just the cruellest smile I have ever seen on a cat."

"Blackmail," said Toby.

"Oh yes," said Vera, "But like nothing I've ever seen - it's a business! If these poor cats leave any little piece of evidence in their room that could cause them trouble, it gets spirited away, stored up, logged against their record for when Corin Fluffs wants to fleece them, or put them under pressure. Happily there was nothing that made sense to me in the clerk's room - I'm sure Grimclaws would have checked to see if I had omitted to mention anything."

"A dangerous business, to bring so many maids in on it in that way."

"Perhaps not so much. All the maids know that they are doing is to collect bits of paper that they find in the rooms. Some of the cleverer ones listen in on conversations too. But if they get caught, it's all deniable. Grimclaws can claim she knew nothing about it, that the maid thought of it for herself. At worst, Fluffs can claim it was down to Grimclaws, or Caché. he is well insulated from it all."

"But if someone like Lucinda had exposed him - she was very well connected. Her refusal to cooperate with his approach was perhaps more dangerous for her." Toby stopped and thought for a moment. "Where are these records kept?"

"Nobody knows. Or rather Fluffs does I suppose, but I don't think it's in the hotel. And most of what is taken away is copied where it can be, and the original returned to the room. Fluffs retains only truly compromising documents where the originals are essential. Beyond that, he simply seems to enjoy having the information - to use when he pleases."

"So perhaps not much actual blackmail goes on?"

"Enough to keep him in the hotel business. They are making enough money to run a luxurious hotel and keep it full while charging barely enough to open half the rooms. But I haven't told you the best of it yet."

"Well?"

"Before I left I dawdled a little at reception, and thanked that reception clerk for his help. He seemed friendly - or at least he wanted to be friendly - and I thought he might know something more. Well, he did. I spotted in the register two names I knew, Danny Alleyfeather and Judge Pennyclaw. Alleyfeather was checking in today - he arrived about 4 o' clock. But Pennyclaw arrived yesterday."

Toby clapped his paws down on the table. "What are those two doing here? Surely not in it together? Or has Fluffs somehow sensed our presence and drawn them here as a distraction? It cannot be coincidence that two of our early suspects are here just as a second murder occurs. We must speak to them."

"You haven't heard the strangest thing yet," said Vera, "The very best suite on the top floor is listed as occupied, but in fact it is only used occasionally. It is simply kept available for the hotel's most important customer, who doesn't even pay for the room. "

"And that is?"

"His Royal Highness, Prince Hector"

22

A NEW LIST OF SUSPECTS

The hubbub of speculation that followed Vera's words had to be quieted by Toby. Since the Prince recruited us to have words with Lucinda, we had not seen him, and indeed a curt note from the Palace had made it clear that our services were no longer required. But we had never completely eliminated him from our list of suspects. Should we now reconsider the possibility? Toby ordered a round of cold milk and cooled our speculative fevers.

"It is no surprise to me that the Prince holds a set of rooms ready as a private retreat. No doubt all the best hotels in Brighton were no sooner made aware of his wishes, than they were competing for the honour of providing for him. I suspect that in this case promises of absolute discretion, and a free room, won out over more traditional establishments. But really it doesn't change anything about our problem. And in fact it does not make him a more likely suspect - only a more likely victim. We probably should warn him away from the Grand Hotel for his own good, but I hardly think he could have been sneaking out of the Red Windmill this afternoon. Hector is a highly conspicuous figure. No, I am more concerned with Vera's other findings. Why have both Judge Pennyclaw and Danny Alleyfeather returned to Brighton just now? Why them and not the Bishop? We need some facts. Robbie, which of them did you think the most trustworthy?"

"Alleyfeather, without a doubt. He has been open with us about what happened, he truly cared for Lucinda, I am sure of that."

"Very well, let us begin with him. We need to find out why he is here, whether Fluffs has drawn him in somehow. But we cannot meet him at the hotel. Vera, would you recognise him?"

"I think so - I have only seen his photograph printed in the Times, but he is a handsome fellow."

"Perhaps I should go?" I offered.

"Robbie, you have been very firmly warned away from the hotel by Corin Fluffs. I think we can trust Vera to one last mission for us. There is no reason to suppose that her story has yet been discovered. Vera, tell Alleyfeather to meet Robbie and myself at the Racecourse tomorrow - there will be a huge crowd and we can blend in easily without fear of discovery. We shall wait at the rails by the third jump in the third race."

"I will. Don't worry Surgeon, I don't much like politicians," and so saying, Vera blew me a kiss before running back off up the length of the pier.

Toby enjoyed staring at my startled face for a moment, before returning to the tangled threads of the mystery.

Gertie patted me kindly, then began, "Tell me again about the four names on Lucinda's list. These four were special to her somehow?"

"The Crown, Parliament, the Law and the Church. Let us call them the four Pillars of the establishment. I think that is what they represented for her - in the person of four very fallible male cats. I think she laughed to herself that they were all so besotted with her, in their different ways, and enjoyed teasing them a little with her power over them. No more than that. So far as I can tell, there was no real attempt at blackmail, and indeed, no real relationship with any of them. The affection went all one way."

"So who did Lucinda love then?"

"I am no longer sure that she cared truly for anyone but herself."

"Never think that, Toby. Miss Redclaw said that she loved to laugh. Though whoever laughed at

Buttons and Bells will do it no more. Do you no longer think that one of those four killed her - are you quite determined that Fluffs is somehow at the bottom of this?"

So challenged, Toby arranged his thoughts aloud for us, showing the elegant order of his mind.

"There are four possible sets of suspects I can see here: One of Lucinda's past or present friends, of whom the four we have just mentioned seem most likely; Some colleague at the Red Windmill. But the second killing has narrowed our field of suspects there considerably - it seems that just Victoria Gingersnap or Miss Redclaw could be concerned."

"Or Mittens," I added.

Toby ignored me and carried on. "Or possibly Corin Fluffs and his gang are somehow at the bottom of it. I would almost like that to be the answer, only it would be the very devil to prove. Or else some mysterious person from her past - an old friend or family member perhaps has tracked Lucinda down. An old sin, with a long shadow. Now as to motive, for the Pillars, this would have been a crime essentially to avoid embarrassment, exposure of some kind. A loss of face, perhaps a lost career. This motive was strongest for the Prince, but disappeared in smoke as soon as we met Lucinda. Unless some third party also threatened him with exposure, perhaps that could bring us back to Corin Fluffs again. Bishop Redfur too had a great deal to lose. He has a high reputation in the church, he has a chance of becoming Archbishop one day. He did lie to us about his dealings with her."

"Ah yes!" I started up, "he pretended to have last seen her in March, when in fact he had an appointment to see her again on the 20th of May."

Gertie joined in, "Could there be an explanation there for an attack on Victoria? Some religious mania?"

Toby shook his head, "Oddly, the Bishop did not seem to me to be a very religious cat. Yet, yes, there is something peculiar there. Why have the others been assembled in Brighton, and not the Bishop? I should like to know if he left Chichester today."

"I'll find out," I offered.

"Alleyfeather was in love with Lucinda. If he really meant to marry her, and dash his own career to pieces in so doing, then killing her would make no sense. The Judge seemed quite detached about Lucinda, and perhaps would have been least embarrassed. It is not clear that any of that group had a real motive. But our strongest suspect for now seems to be the Bishop."

"What about the Prince?" asked Gertie.

"Certainly there was a strong motive to avoid embarrassment - his forthcoming wedding. But he engaged us for that very reason, and Lucinda conceded instantly. Unless some darker motive is at play, I cannot consider him a serious suspect."

"And your second group of suspects - the players at the Windmill?"

Gertie interrupted me. "You can rule them out - assuming the same killer attacked Richard as Lucinda, then the only ones with opportunity are Victoria and Miss Redclaw. The former is so vain she thinks she was the intended victim, the latter would never have harmed Lucinda, I am quite certain of it."

"Could Corin Fluffs be to blame?" I asked "He could perhaps have been taking some kind of revenge on Lucinda for refusing to take part in his blackmailing ring. Or she may have been capable of exposing his plans in some way, she certainly had powerful connections who would have listened to her. But again we have no firm evidence. So far as we know, he is merely coincidentally in the way."

"What did you mean by the last possibility - someone from Lucinda's past?" Gertie asked, looking intently at Toby.

"We don't know very much about her origins, nothing whatever about her family, nor even her time before coming to Brighton. It could be that someone from that past has tracked her down, or stumbled upon her again after a long interval, and for some reason we know nothing of, felt driven to kill her."

"But why kill Richard too?"

"I suspect, Gertie, that if we only knew the answer to that, we should know that answer to all of our questions about this crime, the how, the who and the why."

23
A DAY AT THE RACES

The next day was a Friday. It was race day, and we formed quite a jolly party heading up to the racecourse on the hills over Brighton. It is a fashionable business, and the ladies were dressed in quite enormous hats, so decked about with flowers and ribbons that their faces were half obscured. Although we went up early to be there at the start, the course was thronged. Brighton is a popular racecourse, and the turnstiles were jammed full of cats and dogs of every class, pressing to get in. The racing of horses is one of the very few sports which seems to hold an equal appeal to the feline and canine worlds, and long gone are the dark days of segregation in the lead up to the Great Wars. Still of course most restaurants remain separate, as the difference in our palates is so great. We headed for the finest of the feline restaurants, to choose a light lunch and watch the first race. It was interesting to watch the mingled crowds below, clusters of dogs in their families, cats in theirs. The upper classes of dog and cat circulated together in the high enclosure behind the red ribbons whilst the working dogs and cats of every kind who could take a day's holiday and afford a ticket thronged the rails about the course. Perhaps it is not so much class as money that makes the difference, although dogs take note of pedigrees just so much as our 'blue blood' cats do. I observed some fine-boned greyhounds sniffing at each other, and curled and glossy setters resisting the urge to scamper along.

We sat at our table which was spread with a fine white cloth and were brought mackerel paste with biscuits, and a light lemon-scented tea. The horses were assembled for the first race, their nostrils flared with anticipation. Each was backed by a jockey-cat, his or her head topped with a bright silk cap in the owner's colours. These were tiny cats, fitted for their trade by their physique and ability to cling to a bolting horse. The favourite in the first race was a horse called 'Pegasus', who looked more like a black devil than his namesake. He seemed to be sweating already, and a fine foam trickled around his mouth. The jockey on top was a young molly with blue-grey fur and white socks. Her cap was bright blue and white, and she looked grimly anxious as she clung to the bucking horse. Once all the horses were locked inside the metal pens at the start, the officials climbed up on either side, and at the starter's pistol, pulled hard on the ropes to release the gate. It flew upwards on the pulleys, and the horses darted out, with clods of earth and grass flying out from their hooves as they raced away. Pegasus seemed not to have got away well, taking a kick from a neighbouring brown horse, but he soon pulled away, overtaking the field, and easily won in the single lap of the course.

We ran down to the winner's enclosure, where a beaming owner, in an ill-fitting top hat, clasped the winner's trophy, a wild-eyed Pegasus attempted to take bites out of his adoring crowd, and the jockey continued to cling. Just at that moment, my paw was clutched by a very short ginger cat beside me, who I had at first taken for a young kit, and he pulled me down to whisper in my ear.

"Are you that detective cat?" he asked in a hoarse voice.

"I have the honour to be the friend of the great Toby Hunter," I replied. "Did you want to meet him?"

"Not now" the cat replied, "I'll meet you here after the last race".

Before I could say another word he was gone, disappeared into the crowd. I turned back but Toby and the ladies were already returning to our table to watch the second race. I hurried after them, and informed Toby of this strange approach.

"Curious," he said. "Do you think he has some connection to the case?"

"I can't quite see what horse racing has to do with blackmail and dancers, but if you want to meet him then I suppose we shall find out!" We were served with glasses of sparkling honeysuckle wine and fine crumble cake. As the horses lined up for the race, I was startled to see my new acquaintance atop a bay horse, and discovered his name from my programme.

"That is Timothy Bobbins, the jockey!" I declared, "He is riding Flashing Star today, for the Earl Greyfur."

"Well, well - a racing matter then?"

"I know of Greyfur - he has had a terrible run of luck this last six months, he cannot seem to win a race. This right after his Manchester cotton factory burned to the ground. Bobbins has been his jockey for five years" said Gertie

"I didn't know you were a racing fan?' said Hunter, surprised.

"Oh I find it most interesting," said Gertie. "Not just the races themselves, but the whole world connected with it; such an interesting mixture of cats - and dogs - that come to the courses. And when one understands a little of the background, the 'form' of a horse, the training in the lead up to a race, why then the races are so much more exciting."

"You must be our expert guide then. What have you heard about Bobbins?"

"The rumours abound, but some have suggested that he has put on too much weight and this is slowing the horses."

I looked again at the tiny cat, clinging grimly to the enormous bay racehorse, Flashing Star, as it twisted its neck to try and bite him. "He doesn't exactly look portly!" I said.

"The jockeys all stay very thin - it is unclear how much difference it makes to the horses, but it seems to be a matter of pride with them. Bobbins was one of the best. He won the Gold Cup one year on one of Earl Greyfur's horses. Myself I suspect something else lies behind the recent trouble."

"Such as?" enquired Toby.

"There has been some interference with the races, I suspect. I think it would be of interest to look at the betting on them. Who has been profiting from Earl Greyfur's losses?"

We turned back to the race just as the gate flew up, and the horses bolted away. Bobbins made great efforts, screaming into his horse's ear to spur him on, but was beaten by three others, and gained nothing for his trouble. He looked deeply downcast. Finally it was time for the third race, and we left the ladies lunching and made our way to the rail. Alleyfeather joined us just as the race began, and we had to shout at each other over the roar of the crowd.

"What do you want?" he demanded, crossly

"Why are you here?"

"At the racecourse? Because you asked me to come!" he spat back.

"Don't be obtuse. Why have you come back to Brighton?"

"Because you asked me to come. Really, Hunter, this is beyond a joke!" So saying, Alleyfeather fished a note still in its grey envelope out of his waistcoat pocket, and handed it to Toby.

He read it with a wry smile and passed it to me. In capital letters, it read

'COME TO BRIGHTON AT ONCE, VITAL INFORMATION FOR YOU. TOBY HUNTER'

24
THE JOCKEY'S TALE

Alleyfeather told us he had received the note, marked 'Personal' at his Parliamentary offices, a few days before. He had cleared his diary as best he could, and headed smartly to the coast. He knew no more. We told him what had happened to Richard Greywhiskers, and he looked deeply troubled.

"But this has been done to incriminate me!" he cried. The cheers rang out ironically from the stands behind us, as the favourite romped home. Toby and I could not help but agree.

"I fear it does look bad for you," said Toby, although I think the police have not yet made the connection, you are now implicated in both murders.

"Wait," said Danny, holding up a paw, "I must think." We waited.

"What time was Greywhiskers killed? It was yesterday, you said?"

"Yes, at about three o clock."

"Well then I am in the clear for once! My train did not get in until half past three, then I went straight to the hotel."

"That would tally, a witness saw you arrive there at four."

"What's going on, Hunter?" asked Danny, cleaning his whiskers abstractedly. "I am somehow clinging to my job, but I feel as if someone is determined to destroy me. And I saw that old reprobate Pennyclaw at the hotel too."

Hunter gave him a sharp look. "Ah did you indeed? And how do you come to be staying at the Grand Hotel? Did you by any chance get offered an excellent rate for your stay?"

"Yes, an offer arrived for all members of Parliament - it was by much the same post as this note. I thought it rather fortunate, but perhaps it was more sinister."

"It seems we cannot be of much help to one another today. I advise you to leave quickly. But if you should think of anything else, let us know. And please keep in touch."

"Where could I run to?" said Danny with a sad smile. I am rather too well known, don't you think?"

We left him staring listlessly over the racing rail at the torn-up ground, and strolled back to the restaurant. Gertie and Vera had observed our conversation with interest, and without a word Toby handed the note to Gertie.

"Ah - not really from you, I take it."

"No" said Toby, "And I should not be surprised to learn that Pennyclaw has another like it. The Prince lives in Brighton, so he need not have been lured, but..."

"Speak of Cerberus" muttered Vera, and pointed to the Royal Enclosure.

A plump Prince Hector had appeared, wearing an outlandish bright purple cape, and matching cap, in grotesque imitation of a jockey. He could have made four of Timothy Bobbins, but he was clearly being fawned upon and congratulated on his outfit by the little group around him. A number of dignitaries clustered about behind the purple tape, and I was surprised to see Danny Alleyfeather amongst them, bowing low over Hector's paw.

"Politicians are never off-duty," remarked Vera "There is always someone to be won over to their point of view."

Fairpaw, the sad, thin tabby cat we had seen an aeon ago at the Palace had somehow made his way into the enclosure, and we observed him pulling at the Prince's cape for a moment, in a vain effort to be heard, before he was ejected, tail first.

The last race was about to start. This was to be over three laps of the course; Pegasus, Flashing Star, and the Prince's horse, Conquest, were racing, alongside three others. We watched the little pack line up in the gates, Pegasus clashing his hooves against the metal in eagerness to be off. The jockeys bobbed up and down like so many boats tossed on a stormy sea. A hush fell, the pistol rang out, and the horses bolted away. We watched them closely with narrowed eyes as they tore away around the first corner, jostling closely, far too close. A scream rang out and we saw a dark horse fall, rolling on the ground close to its jockey, who barely escaped with her life. The rest of the field continued around the back of the course, too far away to be sure who was in the lead, but as they rounded back towards us again, we saw Flashing Star just leading, neck stretched out, mane flying, and Bobbins crouched flat against the horse's neck. But close beside her was Conquest, a pure white horse, with wild wide eyes. She panted for breath as she thundered past, jockeyed by a young white female cat who could barely be seen save for her purple cap. It was the Prince's conceit to partner a white horse with a white jockey, but his aides served him well, and the pair were racing to win.

Three other horses followed half a length behind, but there was no sixth. It was Pegasus who had fallen, and he cantered along much later, jumping over the fence and off across the fields, pursued by his furious jockey. For the second turn of the course, Flashing Star and Conquest remained neck and neck, joined for half the course by a third horse from the pack, named General Blue, owned by an aristocratic greyhound from the Bluenose family, but jockeyed by a tabby cat. Still Flashing Star pulled just ahead, by the length of his nose. They turned away, and the last two horses, both focused on the pack ahead, stumbled into each other, leaving only those three in the race. Something happened on the straight stretch on the far side of the course. A shout rang out, taken up by the crowd, as Flashing Star began to fall back. Conquest and General Blue thundered on, first one then the other ahead, around the final turns of the course. Along with half the crowd on the course, we hurried down to the rails to cheer them in. As they came towards us no one could tell which was first. The crowd held its breath, but as they crossed the line Conquest dipped her neck a fraction more, and crossed the line ahead. A huge roar went up, betting tickets and hats thrown in the air like confetti, and finally Flashing Star limped in, a sad two lengths behind them.

Gertie pointed out Earl Greyfur up in the enclosure, grimly tearing up his betting slips, and grinding them into the ground. The Prince was delighted, and jumped over the purple tape of the enclosure, calling over his greyhound rival and clapping him on the back. He remained dignified and nodded politely, but was persuaded to share the prize. Prince Hector had a winning way with the crowds of both species, that gave his family some hope for a prosperous future. I noticed at last a thin, pale looking cat by his side, a sparkling chain of diamonds laced about her head.

"Princess Alexandrina," Vera whispered to me. "Poor thing. I daresay she had little to do with the arranging of this marriage. He hardly seems her type."

Indeed, though I deplored Vera's way of talking about a Royal lady, Alexandrina looked weary already, looking without enthusiasm at the joyful crowds, and fatly laughing aristocats clustered about her fiancé. She retreated to a bench in the shade and fanned herself, as he strode up to take the trophy. The crowds had drifted away from the rails and up to the parade ring, where Fifi, the Prince's jockey, was wreathed in smiles. However we stayed put and sure enough Timothy Bobbins came up to us, nodding at Toby and myself in tacit conspiracy.

"You have to help me" he cried.

"I'm no trainer of horses. I don't even know much about racing!" laughed Toby.

Bobbins looked close to tears. "This ain't racing! Not as I'm used to it. That horse ought to be winning. It's the best one out there by far, saving maybe Pegasus on his best days, but it seems that every race something goes wrong. It isn't me! But the Earl won't stand for it much longer. He'll let me go, and then what shall I do? I'm too young to stop racing. It's my life!"

"Slow down!" said Toby "What are you saying?"

"Someone is doping that horse." said Bobbins, in a low voice. "It isn't me, but it has to be someone at the yard, someone that can see the horse on a race day. I'm sure the Earl suspects me of something."

"Why would you hobble your own mount?" I asked, bemused. Bobbins looked at me scornfully. I shouldn't do it, not ever. But there are some as do. They can make money betting against themselves. It's a wicked business, but it's not unheard of in horse racing. It's been going on too long though."

"What do you want me to do?" asked Toby

"Just find out who it is, stop them, and let me win races again!" cried Bobbins.

"Oh is that all? Very well we shall do our best. But I am a private detective, can you pay?" Bobbins pulled a gold medal out of his pocket.

"Take this" he said. "If it goes on this way much longer I shan't be proud of it any more." It was the Gold Cup medal.

25
THE PAINTER AND THE BISHOP

Toby accepted Bobbins' commission, though not the medal. We were eager to leave the racecourse, for in our two lines of enquiry we now needed to find Earl Greyfur, the Bishop of Chichester and Judge Pennyclaw. But as we left, we passed the dejected figure of Fairpaw, slumped on the ground and rubbing his paws in the litter of dirt and discarded betting slips. Toby and I exchanged a look, and I crouched down beside the despondent figure.

"Might I ask how you are acquainted with Prince Hector?"

"If only I had been acquainted with him." muttered Fairpaw in a low growl. "I should have known then, that unlike the gentlecat I supposed him to be, he would not pay me for my work."

"What work was that?" asked Toby.

Fairpaw looked up, narrowing his eyes against the sun.

"Have you seen the ceiling frescoes in his audience chamber? Tigers chasing the phoenix through a jungle. My best work."

"You painted that? Why it is a quite remarkable work!" This was true enough, though not all remarks upon it would be favourable. Still, it was no doubt all a piece with Hector's taste.

"How can it be that you have not been paid?"

Fairpaw laughed bitterly. "Because the Phoenix, Sir, is not a blue bird."

"What?"

"I painted it blue - why not? There is no such beast, and it seemed to me to go well with the scheme. The colour made a great contrast with the orange of the tiger. But it seems that Prince Hector is of the opinion that a Phoenix is yellow. He will not pay me, though I worked myself into a great debt in the six months it took me. And now what shall I do? I have not even ten pennies to buy more paint."

He curled himself into a ball, and sobbed.

Toby reached into his pocket and pulled out a gold coin, dropping it into Fairpaw's discarded hat. "I think we have accrued rather more of the Prince's wealth than we have fairly earned. Take this and welcome to it."

Fairpaw thanked us, and we set off to find our quarry, wondering at the folly of our Royal employer.

The Bishop we tracked down in a church.

"A pleasure to see you again, Bishop" hailed Toby.

The Bishop looked as if it was anything but a pleasure to him, and indeed perhaps Toby had forgotten the rather tense way in which we had parted in Chichester. However Bishop Redfur recollected at least his usual urbane manner, and greeted us with a smile. His words did not entirely match his manner.

"What do you want? I managed to find a reasonable explanation for an urgent visit to Brighton, but it is hardly convenient. Luckily the vicar of this fine establishment wished to consult me about some theological matters, however it is a business I could usually have managed in correspondence."

"Yet you came" remarked Toby, mildly.

"I did. Your note..."

"It was not my note."

"Whatever do you mean?" Redfur pulled out a neatly folded square of paper from inside his clawbook and brandished it at Toby. "Do you deny having written this? Remember to whom you are speaking!"

"How can I forget?" laughed Toby, dipping his head in mockery of a nosegreeting. "But I'm afraid you have been hoaxed, Bishop. That note was not from me, and I fear you are one of a number of Lucinda's old acquaintances who has been so fooled."

Redfur fell silent for a moment, and folded the note away.

"Then that is why the Judge is here? I ran into him in the street this morning and he claimed to be on a visit to some friend at the local assizes, but I thought it strange. Great Bast when will I be free of this? Did I do so very wrong?"

The second question Toby wisely ignored, but dared to answer the first. "I fear that you will not be 'free' of this matter until we can lay hands on the murderer of Lucinda Lexington. Can you do any more to help us in that? What happened when you saw her in May?"

Redfur cast a regretful look behind him, but the vicar was out of hearing and merely waved a friendly paw.

"I had to see her about her letter."

"She wrote to you?"

"Yes, it was most unladylike. She threatened to make more of our acquaintance than there had been, to embarrass me in my diocese."

"Are you sure? She does not seem actively to have blackmailed any other cat. Merely to have amused herself with them. What did she want?"

"Oh. Well, I suppose there was no specific request as such."

"Did you keep the letter?"

"No. I ... I burned it."

"This may be important. Can you remember exactly what it said?" The Bishop looked very thoughtful.

"You know it is strange, at the time I was perhaps rather panicked, but thinking back I wonder if it was quite such a threatening letter as I imagined. It was quite a short note, something like, 'Dearest Redfur, I miss your conversation, do come and see me when you can, or shall I have to find you in Chichester' "

"That was all?" I shouted.

The vicar, who had been quietly arranging flowers on the altar, looked up sharply and took a step towards us. Redfur waved him away.

"Yes," he whispered. "That was all. But you cannot blame me for taking it amiss, receiving such a familiar letter from a lady in her line of work."

"Singing and dancing" observed Toby. "Yes, it must have been most alarming, given your position."

"Well quite" said the Bishop. "So I went to see her."

"And?"

Redfur scratched nervously at his bright stole. "She - laughed at me. She said I had nothing to fear, but that it was nice to know she could get my attention when she wanted it. She was very rude."

"How annoying for you. But that was her only 'price' - she wanted to be able to talk to you?" The Bishop took a glance back at the vicar, who was no longer wholly absorbed in his flowers, and escorted us up the aisle towards the doors of the church.

"I meet a lot of different cats in my calling, and I had thought myself a good judge of character. In her case I had been mistaken. I thought she was a lost soul in need of a little guidance, someone with whom I could do some good. Instead I think now that she never really liked me. I think she was a collector."

"Of what?"

"Persons of influence. She liked to know the people who counted, to be able to walk up to them and claim acquaintance in a crowd. And she did not like to lose anyone from her collection."

"And did she have anything else to say when you last parted, on the 20th May?"

"She advised me to consider the state of my soul!"

I was quite unable to stifle a chuckle at this.

"One more question" said Toby, "Where did you meet her?"

"At her apartment in Brighton. I followed her there from the Windmill."

"And she was alone?"

" I thought so at first, but when I raised my voice to her that awful comedian emerged from another room and showed me out. "

"Comedian? Who do you mean?"

"Buttons. He half threw me down the stairs!"

26

EARL GREYFUR OF FIRLE

Earl Greyfur had a great house near Lewes, so having left a note for Judge Pennyclaw at the Grand Hotel, we set out to find the Earl by dog-cart. It was a beautiful journey, through a patchwork of green fields to the north-east of Brighton, but a wasted trip, as a butler at the very gate of the grand estate informed us that the noble Earl was at his trainer's place near Rottingdean. We duly returned south to Rottingdean, and made the greyhound's day with a double fare. He tied up his cart outside the Black Horse inn and sloped in to raucous greetings from his fellow cabbies. We walked on through the village, stopping only for elegant refreshment at the very dignified Plough Inn, run by a tall black cat of few words. We sat for a little while in the warm sun, supping our nipbeer, and admiring the ducks bobbing about on the pond. Just up the hill from the village, heading away from the coast, was a set of fields filled with horses, some galloping about freely, and some under training. We shortly reached the ridge of the hill, and stopped to watch for a while, as a jockey galloped along on a jet black steed. After a while I noticed a slight cat also leaning against the fence some hundred yards down from us, and recognised the Earl himself.

"There, Toby he is watching the gallops!" I declared.

"No, he isn't," said Toby, who had been watching him for some time.

The Earl's head was looking, not out at the galloping horses, but down, at his own paws clawing on the fence. We padded over to greet him.

"A fine day for the gallops!" cheered Toby. "Earl Greyfur, is it not?"

"I have that honour" answered the Earl. "Who do I have the pleasure of addressing?"

He had the ancient aristocatic custom of an excessive civility of speech, not necessarily matched in actions.

"May I introduce my companion, Surgeon Robert Gentlepaws, and I am Toby Hunter."

"And you, Sir, are not a Surgeon, I take it."

"I am a private detective."

"Then what can your business be with me? I am generally alone here, watching my horses, and I candidly admit that is my preference."

"It is about your horses, Earl, that I have taken the liberty of approaching you. They seem to have lost a few more races than one might expect of late."

"And what in Cerberus' name business is it of yours if they have? My horses have nothing to do with anyone else." The civility was gone.

"I fear I must take issue with you there. Your trainer must be affected when the horses from his stable cease to perform, your jockeys must begin to lose their reputations, and of course, those who back your horses to win must suffer - at least - some disappointment."

The Earl snorted, rather like a horse. "You do not mean to tell me, I suppose, that some disgruntled gambler has engaged you."

"I do not mean to tell you anything about my client, my dear Earl, only to point out that many cats might have an interest in the running of your horses besides yourself."

The Earl recovered somewhat of his patrician manner. "I hope you will concede, however, Mister Hunter, that no one can be more interested than myself. And I find myself at a loss. Sometimes, notoriously so in fact, one has a bad run of luck at this game. Often there is no particular reason for it. No doubt if you were more acquainted with the world of racing you would know that. I shall thank you in the meantime not to trouble me any further. Perhaps my luck will change soon, and your client can rest easy."

"Let us hope so."

The Earl walked away, pausing only to stroke the nose of a fine bay horse who was still panting from his hard ride, and to nod at the jockey, a small female cat. I moved to go, but Toby pressed my paw, so we waited until the jockey had turned the horse and also begun to head away. Toby swooped down and snatched up a small object from the ground, hard by the fence, then walked rapidly back down the hill. I followed. I asked him what he had found, but he hissed at me for silence until we had regained the village, and found a quiet corner at the Black Horse inn.

Largely surrounded by cabbie hounds, we felt confident we could not be overheard here, and found out a cosy snug between the two main bars. The Black Horse is perhaps the most ancient inn in the village of Rottingdean (although there are several, and many are worth the trip to the coast), and is believed to retain its original Yooman name. The great beams holding up the roof are black with age, and the windows are left artistically dark with grime. The Labrador landlord brought us two mugs of warm milk, and accepted our coins without a word, pausing only to pull shut the door of the snug. Disregarding the raucous barks from the adjacent rooms I could but admire our cosy surroundings, with a few bright cushions on the silkily worn wooden benches, and portraits of famous smugglers, both feline and canine, on the walls.

"Well, what was it?" I demanded, as soon as our host had gone. Toby held out a small apple. I laughed.

"That's the worst clue I've ever seen! Even I know that a doting owner likes to feed his horses apples and carrots. You cannot be making much of that?"

"Take a closer look" said Toby.

I picked up the apple and took it over to the window. At first it seemed quite unremarkable, until I noticed a ring carved into the surface of it on one side. I glanced back at Toby and he nodded. I dug a claw into this carved ring and pulled; a chunk fell out of the apple. Beneath this plug a hollow had been carved out, and a small blue pill was there. I shook it out and held it up to the light. I didn't know what drug it was, but I could guess its purpose.

"The horses are being doped!" I declared angrily. "This is a devilish business. We must show this to the Earl."

"I rather think the Earl knows all about it, don't you? I saw him drop this as we approached."

"What? Hobble his own horses? Why would he do such a thing?"

"It is very difficult to make certain of the outcome of a horse race. Impossible, almost, to guarantee a win. But relatively simple to be certain that a favourite will lose."

"The Earl has been betting against his own horses?"

"Yes, I don't doubt it now. I rather think he intends to stop soon. He told us as much. I think he will take my warning. But just to make certain, I might send him a little final advice."

Toby took back the pill from me and snapped it in half. "Get that part analysed, would you Robbie?" he asked, then took out his clawpad, and scribbled a note. He placed the half pill in the centre and folded it up into a billet, then whistled for the landlord. The dog came in and waited respectfully on Toby's instructions.

"Would you be so kind as to find one of your customers who might run this note up to Firle Place for the Earl? No need to bring a reply. And then we shall require a cab into Brighton."

The Labrador looked puzzled. "Are you gentlecats not here to meet Mr Fluffs, then?" My face must have instantly given us away, but in a flash Toby leapt up in front of me. "No I fear we really cannot wait any longer. Please tell him we were sorry to miss him."

The Labrador nodded slowly and called out to the now very raucous room. Our greyhound of the earlier trip pulled himself away, still laughing, and we had a very rapid, though unsteady trip back into Brighton.

27
THE JUDGEMENT OF PENNYCLAW

At our hotel, a small townhouse in the Lanes, we found Judge Pennyclaw waiting for us in the lobby. He was much mellowed, having absorbed some third of a bottle of honeysuckle wine in the wait.

"For someone so anxious for my presence you have taken your time in coming" he muttered.

"Ah, but I fear it was not I who requested your presence, Judge. At least, not at first," said Toby.

"Must you always speak in riddles? What a very tiresome cat you are. You should get very short shrift in my courtroom y'know. Come and have some of this wine, anyway, it's first rate, and your hotelier has some excellent little biscuits that have just the right amount of salt in them."

We sat comfortably, and I must admit it was a very pleasant little interview amidst all our unpleasant matters. I addressed myself to the biscuits and wine, while Toby addressed himself to the Judge.

"You have been fooled, Judge. Someone has forged notes to a number of Lucinda's acquaintances, and brought them to Brighton on pretext that I wanted to see them."

Pennyclaw sat down his drink, lay back in his chair, and clicked his pawclaws together, in the attitude of judgement for which his court was famous. He thought, then spoke.

"Who has been summoned in this way?"

"Aside from yourself, Bishop Redfur and Danny Alleyfeather. Prince Hector was in any case in Brighton."

"And what do you consider to be the significance of this?"

"The timing was important. There has been another death."

The Judge sat upright abruptly. "Who?"

"Richard Greywhiskers."

"The comic, he was also known as Buttons," I added.

Pennyclaw leapt out of his chair and took a turn about the room. "This is very bad" he muttered. "Someone is trying to frame me!"

"Something of that kind," said Toby. "Although it seems that our murderer does not much care which of you is implicated, so long as it is one of you."

"It's an outrage," he snarled. "Just wait 'til this comes to trial!"

"I rather think that if it does, you might be advised not to try it yourself."

"Hmph. Well, and what are you doing about it?" Toby also stood, and paced over to the window.

"It has not been a simple matter. Corin Fluffs is here, and is up to some devilry - blackmail I think. It has been somewhat tangled up with that, and it has distracted me. But I think that I begin to see my way. What do you remember about Richard Greywhiskers?"

"Nothing. He always seemed to be in the way, hanging about Lucinda. A little over-fond of her, a little protective perhaps?"

"Bishop Redfur told us that Buttons was at Lucinda's apartment when he once visited there."

"Did he indeed? Well it doesn't surprise me. The cat used to follow her around. And I told you before that he gave young Alleyfeather rather a scratch. But there's nothing in that, surely. And if it is he who is dead, then he cannot have been your murderer?"

I burst in with an idea of my own. "Why not? If one of you was quite smitten with Lucinda, and discovered that Richard had killed her, could you not have taken revenge?"

The Judge gave me a rather scornful look. "Revenge? Great Hound, what trashy magazines have you been reading? The cat told awful jokes, and played the fool. I can't see him strangling Lucinda to death and in any case for what reason?"

"Jealousy?" I muttered weakly.

"Tchah!" spat Pennyclaw. "If he was as close an observer of Lucinda as I think, then he will have known there was nothing really to be jealous of. And in any case I think she was quite as fond of him as of anyone else."

"What makes you think that?" asked Toby.

"Oh just an impression."

"Impressions are formed by observations. Conscious or unconscious. Think harder, what did you see?"

Pennyclaw nodded and resumed his seat. He closed his eyes and breathed deeply, remembering. His eyes flicked open.

"I saw them give a nosegreeting one day. Just as I was arriving. It was only for a second, and they both turned away, as if embarrassed. But it was clearly affectionate. Still, I don't see how that helps. More confusion. He can't be a suspect, and even if he were, he cannot have contrived his own murder. It gets you no further."

"Not at all," said Toby. "In fact you have both helped me. You have hit on something there, Surgeon."

"Really? You think it could have been Buttons who killed Lucinda?"

"Think Robbie, how did he seem when we first met him?" I tried to recall that day at the Windmill. My head filled with a vision of Victoria Gingersnap, floating like a bird through the air, wreathed about with the gyrating banners of the ribbon dancers.

Toby smiled at me, seeming to read my thoughts, and asked gently "What did Richard Greywhiskers do, and what did he tell us?"

I tried to picture the scene, the Windmill troupe gathered about in front of the stage. Buttons had been there, but I could not recall him saying anything except to tell us about his altercation with Danny Alleyfeather. I said as much.

"Exactly," said Toby, with a grin. "He did nothing to draw attention to himself, but when he spoke it was to draw our attention to someone else entirely. What else, Robbie, what was his mood, do you think?"

"He was a comic, but he seemed sad."

"And now we begin to see why."

"We do?" I sighed. I took another biscuit from the tray. In fact it was the last. Judge Pennyclaw reached out a second later and was disappointed to find them gone. Instead he poured out a final glass of the honeysuckle wine. Toby surveyed us both with the manner of a teacher sadly disappointed in his pupils.

"I have a little job for Gertie" he said, and ran out of the door.

28
STARS OF THE PHOENIX

Extract from the journal of Gertude Fluff

Toby had requested me this time to carry out an investigation in London. The key to our mystery might lie somewhere in Lucinda's past. He seemed to know something of my connection to it. Although I never can tell with Toby if he really knows things, or simply gets one to admit them by hinting that he does. At any rate, he flattered me that I was the only cat he could trust with this mission, and Toby's flattery is irresistible to me. I began where I had last worked with Lucy, as she then was, at the Phoenix Theatre. I had travelled as Georgina Blackeyes, which served to swing open the theatre doors. I explained that as well as considering a new role on the London stage, I was trying to find traces of my old friend. Although the ownership had changed since my day, they kept a filing cabinet of staff records, including an old home address for Lucy. They kindly directed me to this, and to a few others of our former colleagues.

I found Lucy's old home without too much difficulty. At least I found the address, but every house that had once been on the street had been torn down, and a new row of terraced houses was taking its place. I gleaned from one of the residents that the house in question had been a boarding house, mainly frequented by actresses and artists. The former landlady had got 'new for old' and now lived in the largest house on the corner of the terrace. She had little to add to what I already knew of Lucy, saving that she had never been visited by any family. She thought that Lucy had been an orphan. That would certainly have fitted with Lucy's adoption of the harsh Redclaw as a substitute parent. There are not many orphanages in London, and I struck lucky.

Lucy's place had been the Bluecoat Home near Westminster, but she had run away as a teenager. Her parents had been theatre folk who died in a shipwreck whilst taking the coastal route between theatres. She had a few siblings but they had found other homes and not kept in touch. She had been alone in following the stage.

I went next to track down one of her friends and room mates from the Phoenix. This was Miss Silvia Startail (not, I think, her natural name). Silvia was a beautiful chocolate brown cat, shining dark brown eyes blinking at me from deep set, slanted sockets. We gave one another the cautious welcoming nod of professional actresses. She knew me by reputation, my good reputation as an actress that is, and perhaps thought it a useful connection to foster. Silvia was appearing in a dull 'drawing room' play in a theatre on the outskirts of London, and had never to my knowledge been in the west end. Judging by her good looks, she must therefore be a terrible actress.

"You were another friend of Lucy's then? I read about her death in the papers. Quite a shocking business. Was it a burglar?"

"The police seem to think so," I dissembled. "They want to find her relatives but I gather that is not easily done."

"I shouldn't think it was worth doing," scoffed Silvia. "She had no fondness for them, and they didn't care to acknowledge their sister on the stage. Too grand!"

She paused for a calculation. "Had she much money to leave them? We were great friends of course. I am not surprised she remembered me." I recalled only a few mentions of Silvia from Lucy's letters, and those not awash with affection, rather amusement. Still, we are free to remember our relationship with the dead as we would have wished it to be.

"Who else was Lucy friendly with? I lost touch with her rather in recent years."

"Oh well you know what jealousy is amongst actresses, so not many real close friends like ourselves."

I began to wonder if poor Lucy had had a real friend in the world.

"She had a great many admirers of course. I thought she aimed a little high myself, but she would laugh at me for that." No doubt. "...and then Dick Grey hung around her all the time. I don't know how she could bear that. Such a dull cat he is, lives up to his name. You'd never believe he does a comic turn. I think he followed her down to Brighton. Certainly they went at about the same time."

I tried not to show any excitement. "Oh really? What was his stage name?"

"That was it I think - Dick Grey. Terrible act. I only saw it a few times and it was never any better." Of course a comic who cannot raise a laugh will not get put on stage much more than once. So from all this I gathered that Dick Grey was a reasonable comic, Silvia had little sense of humour, had been rather fond of him herself, and was as jealous of his attachment to Lucy as could possibly be. She rapidly confirmed my conclusions.

"Have you seen him at all down there? He must be distraught."

"I saw him, yes."

She brightened immediately. "How was he?"

I couldn't resist it. "The last time I saw him he was dead."

29
THE PRINCE OF CATS

I had for some time held a serious concern about our investigation, which I hesitated to raise with Toby. However his latest disappearing act, leaving me floundering with a sleepy judge, provoked me into action. On his return, I told Toby what I had done.

"When?" I had his full attention at last.

"This evening" I was a little embarrassed. "I must admit I was not entirely expecting that we should be given another appointment so soon, however..."

"Were you not? I knew full well, my friend, that the instant we asked to see the Prince we should be admitted. It is the reason I have not troubled to confront him before now. However, we have our engagement now and I daresay we should keep it!"

For as soon as Toby had gone, and the Judge had fallen fully asleep, I had acted on my concern and gone to leave a letter of enquiry at the Sandcastle, seeking an audience with Prince Hector. I had felt it quite an omission in our investigation that we had not seen him, at least not to speak to, since our very first encounter.

"Perhaps you had better give me your reasoning however, old friend. Why should we harry the Prince just at this juncture? I admit I have been rather distracted by a few other matters; I may well have made a slip."

I feared to tell. It was simply that the others of Lucinda's close acquaintance we had interviewed twice now, and pressed them all hard. I believed in Toby's assessment that the Prince was no killer. Still, the Prince had been left immune, and I knew the look in Toby's eye when he had scrambled away to find Gertie. He was on a trail, and no doubt it was the right one, but what if the Prince held some vital fact on which the whole business turned? It had happened before that a single careless word, idly discarded, had shaped a snare to trap our villain. In short my reasoning was, rather, a feeling, an anxious certainty of something lacking, not the relentless chain of logic which Toby sought. I stumbled my way through some semblance of explanation, while Toby nodded kindly, but then remembered one other good point.

"Also, he should be warned about Fluffs' hotel. We are certain now that he is in the business of blackmail, and Prince Hector has been the victim of that once already."

"No, he only supposed that he might be, but I take your point."

"Well, what if Corin Fluffs held Prince Hector in his claws? What might he not do?"

"I suspect he would be at quite a loss. He could demand money, I dare say, but it is rather the glamour of a Royal connection, entry behind the red velvet ropes which some influence over Prince Hector could offer. Besides, I suspect the Prince would not be amenable to such influence. Although he wished Lucinda to go away, I think in the end that he would have told her to - go to Cerberus - rather than be subject to her whims."

I gave a little cough, and traced a pattern with my claws on the floor.

"Never mind, dear fellow," said Toby. "You are right that we must leave no stone unturned, and Hector is a largish boulder that we have made no effort to shift. Let us go and see him."

Toby was in a suspiciously good mood. He often seemed so after a private talk with Gertie. I wondered that they did not make a match of it; or rather I did not wonder it, but pitied that they could not, as she was a thief.

Our engagement with Prince Hector was for seven o' clock. We had been placed as his final meeting of the day, and he was anxious to change and get to his evening's entertainment. So much Grimes, his butlercat, warned us of, before knocking on the door of the audience chamber, and in response to an angry growl, showing us in.

"What do you want then? Our business is done, I think?" Hector had dispensed entirely with his Royal manner. "Your note suggested that the documents were destroyed, and I think you were well recompensed. Or did you not think so?" Hector glared at Toby with angrily narrowed eyes.

"Your Royal Highness, I can only beg your pardon if this sudden request for an audience has caused you a moment of anxiety on that count. Certainly, the matter on which you originally engaged me to investigate is at an end and can be of no further concern to you."

Hector shifted uncomfortably on his throne, then jumped down.

"Some other matter has arisen?"

"Yes"

"How does it concern me?"

"First I fear I must advise your Highness of a possible danger. I believe that you have recently been made free of rooms at the Grand Hotel?"

"That is not widely known I hope?"

"It is true, though."

"Yes. I have held a card game or two there. This place is a little public, for all its thousand rooms. They are full of servants, you see."

"Then I must warn you your Highness that the Grand Hotel may also be less private than you might find desirable."

"Oh?"

"I am acquainted, very slightly, with the proprietor, Corin Fluffs. I had the misfortune to have some disagreements with him in Egypt recently. He does not have your deepest and best interests at heart."

Hector paced over to the window and stared out.

"Look at that," he growled.

We joined him at the window. It was a magnificent view, floor to ceiling set with dozens of large panes of the finest flat glass. In the pleasure gardens beyond, crowds of cats of every class strolled about the gardens. Fine silk parasols avoided roaring ragamuffins by a whisker. Every sixth eye was turned towards the window, seeking out a glimpse of the Prince. He afforded some lucky recipients a Royal wave. A dozen cats dropped to the ground in low nosegreetings. He turned away with a harsh laugh.

"They love me, they want to see me, they enjoy my gardens, and yet, wouldn't they love to see me shamed. They would decry it, and abhor it, and love to discuss it for a twelvemonth. I cannot ever quite understand my own people. Am I not a real cat? Must I live entirely in this gilded box, scratching at the surface of life? Bah. Very well, your warning is taken, another door is closed to me. I shall not visit the Grand again."

He sat heavily down on his throne. Snatching up a dark drink from the side table, he lapped at it thirstily. It was a clear note of dismissal, and he seemed quite surprised on looking up to find us still there.

"Was there something else?" Hector demanded with an ironical flick of his tail.

"I wanted to beg a favour," said Toby.

Hector answered only with a widened eye.

"I have been investigating the death of Miss Lucinda Lexington. I know that you were fond of her at one time. I wondered if there was some way in which you might assist us to find her killer."

"And what did you conclude?"

"I think you may have some inklings in the matter. Your Highness takes care to be well informed. You ceased to see Lucinda in February, quite soon after you met her. I wondered if you would tell us why."

"I don't like to share my toys." Hector said it with a smile, but it was no doubt the truth.

"You discovered that despite the honour you paid to Miss Lexington with your attention, she continued to be friendly with many other cats."

"Rather impolite I thought it. I invited her to some charity ball, and she had the nerve to prowl off around the room. Seemed to know half the cats there. I didn't like it. It made me feel foolish. I didn't realise however quite how foolish I had been until I got her letter."

"I see. Might I ask if you can recall who else she seemed to know?"

"You seem to know the answers to all your own questions, Mr Hunter. Perhaps you too should take better care how you use a Prince's time."

"My apologies, your Highness. May I wish you congratulations on your coming marriage?"

"You may."

"I think I might also offer you some comfort as to Lucinda's intentions towards you. I can assure you that she never meant any real harm, nor could she have caused you any."

"How is that?"

"Lucinda Lexington was already married."

30
THREE BUTTONS

After Toby's astonishing pronouncement to Prince Hector, I was perhaps fortunately as dumbstruck as His Royal Highness was, and we left in short order. I demanded, however, that Toby should explain his statement forthwith. He chuckled and admitted he was anticipating somewhat the outcome of Gertie's investigation on his behalf.

"I think it to be the only reasonable explanation for Lucinda's behaviour. Only consider, Robbie, she was clearly a cat in constant pursuit of eligible connection, more than one of whom showed a strong romantic interest in her. A member of Parliament said, at least, that he wanted to marry her. Yet she remained single. Why?"

"I hadn't thought of it in that way."

"Nor had I, until you put it in my head with your mention of jealousy. What if she were already married? And who could be more jealous than a husband?"

"But what husband? What, you cannot think that she married one of the 'four pillars'?"

"No. Although I did briefly wonder if that could have been the true nature of Prince Hector's indiscretion. I think instead that she had a husband already in London, some low connection from her past as an aspiring actress, and that this person followed her to Brighton and was persuaded to keep the marriage secret."

"But what husband could agree to such a thing? And then when she - flirted - so outrageously with other cats, why it could not be borne!"

"Certainly not by you, my friend. When you marry you shall proclaim it to the world, as is right and proper. But remember that Lucinda was very persuasive, she may have held the power in this relationship, she was a star of the stage, she may have set the terms on which the marriage was to continue."

"Why not divorce?"

"Why indeed? But there is another possibility I have considered here, which could yet explain all. It could be that another emotion was at play which overpowered all reason. The strongest of all feelings which can drive a cat."

"Love?"

"Yes, and whatever else I am uncertain of, I think Lucinda was killed by love."

"But then who was this mysterious husband? He must at least have been nearby - surely we must have met him."

"We have - I think so at least. Gertie will confirm my suspicions or set me in disarray when she returns. I have asked her to go to the Records Office to seek out the marriage register, but I already am sure who the cat is."

"But who, Toby? Why are we not tracking him down?"

"He has already been overtaken by fate. No, by the Great Cat's paw, I shall eat my own clawbook if she was not married to Richard Greywhiskers."

I was astonished, and yet in the same moment I knew that he spoke the truth. That cat's demeanour when we met him, the sudden fall into dishumour, the reference to his presence at Lucinda's chambers. It all fitted perfectly.

"You think her own husband killed her? Finally driven beyond endurance? But Buttons is also dead. Who then killed him?"

"You go too fast, my friend. If I am right and Buttons was Lucinda's husband, then it explains a great deal. It does not tell us for sure even who killed her."

Gertie appeared to interrupt us. "You were half right. I have two certificates for you" she said Toby took them without a word, and looked grim.

"Then she is in great danger" said Toby.

31

BLACK HOLES AND REVELATIONS

We had to act fast, and headed at once back to Rottingdean. The four of us, Vera, Gertie, Toby and myself, took a pair of cabs, and were quick enough down to the seafront. The cabs bowled along, merrily chasing one another, and dodging around the oncoming traffic, and the holidaymakers darting across the road. The summer was well advanced, but today a grey tinge was creeping into the edges of the clouds. Vera shivered beside me, and I patted her paw for comfort. Toby had bid us all set down at the Black Horse, and so we alighted there. I was reminded of the labrador's words - 'Are you gentlecats not here to meet Mr Fluffs then?'. What could Fluffs have been doing there? It was close enough to the Windmill, certainly; it was our dropping off point, but yet he had seemed not to have been involved in Lucinda's murder. But what of Richard Greywhiskers? Could that have been Fluffs' work? So soon as Toby jumped down from his cab, and Gertie had alighted beside him, I nudged in beside him and whispered in his ear.

"What about Fluffs? Is that why you wanted us to meet here?"

"No need to whisper, Robbie. Gertie here is quite in my confidence as always. Yes, I had not forgotten that Fluffs had been here. A suspicious coincidence, of the kind I never can trust. You will recall the labrador's words?"

I nodded sagely.

"Then you cannot have helped but wonder at them. That he knew Fluffs' name suggests at once that he had been there before, and more than once. Further, they must have had some business to transact, and no doubt of an irregular kind. Yet - the inn seemed prosperous enough; surely the landlord would not risk his name, his business on too dark a matter. What then could it be?"

I nodded much less sagely. My intuition had taken me no further than the first of these conclusions - and that only just now.

"Smuggling," said Toby triumphantly.

"What?"

"Yes, and I curse myself for taking so long to work it out. I think it was you remarked on the legendary tunnels from the village to the shore. That would make sense for the landlord of an inn, and would explain why Fluffs is seen in the pub, but not in the village. It would not surprise me if there were a tunnel to the windmill itself."

"Ah - but surely Fluffs' business is blackmail, not smuggling."

"Fluffs' business, I think, is whatever devilry takes his fancy at the moment. Saving perhaps, murder by his own paw. Still I warrant he found a great convenience in using those smugglers' tunnels, and if he had to become a smuggler to use them - then so be it."

"Oh."

"You have concluded differently?"

"No."

Toby smiled and beckoned us inside the Black Horse. Our companions had gone in ahead of us, and looked round in puzzlement as we followed inside.

"It is really more of a dogs' pub," said Toby apologetically. "Still I know they can accommodate us."

We all four bundled into the snug room between the two main bars, where the noises of barking and laughter were slightly muffled. The labrador himself came by to take our order.

"You two again? Corin Fluffs said ..."

"Ha! he will have his little joke with us, won't he Robbie? I think you will find, Blackie, that we were expected."

"You know my name?" said the dog. "Of course I do. Corin would not send us to meet him and not tell us how to find him, would he now?"

I too had seen Blackie's name on the owner's plaque outside the inn, but it was bold of Toby to use it. Blackie sat down and scratched behind an ear with his hind leg. Quite a vulgar gesture. Happily the ladies did not seem distressed. Indeed I think I heard Vera stifle a laugh.

"You had better come with me. He didn't say anything about no girl-cats though."

"The ladies will be happy to wait here. If you might fetch them some refreshment?"

Blackie barked at a waitress, who scuttled off to fetch sprats and buttermilk. Then he passed through a swing door behind the bar. We followed. We seemed to be in a store room of some kind, raw meats hanging on hooks from the ceiling, and an ice-box in a corner cooling the milk. Blackie clawed away a knotted rug on the floor, to reveal a trap door. He picked up the rope in his teeth and pulled it open. Gray stone hewn steps descended into blackness.

Blackie turned to face us. He bared his teeth in a manner I did not like at all. "I suppose you are quite certain that Mr Fluffs is expecting you? He did say you were not welcome when you came before, and he made no mention of your arrival today."

"Oh Mr Fluffs and I are old sparring companions," I said. This was true enough, though I should not care to spar with him again.

"I suppose he will have told you the password then?"

"Of course," said Toby, without a pause. "It's Lucinda."

This had to be a happy guess, or else there was not really a password. Blackie growled, and went on down into the tunnel. It was a passage cut straight into the chalk, propped up with stout beams at odd intervals. Little piles of chalk rubble littered the way, whether from excavation, or collapses of the roof, I knew not. A strange white mud of chalk dust clung to the fur and clogged inbetween my toes. Here and there lamps were nailed into the walls. Blackie lit them as we went from a tinder box he scraped at with his great claws. As we approached each lamp, his matt fur blended into the darkness beyond, and only his great brown eyes glinted in the gloom.

The confined space and the darkness heightened my senses, and my head was filled with the ancient terror.

'Be not alone with Dog,' cried the primitive part of my brain. The scent of damp fur filled my nostrils. I could scent Toby's fear too. The passage descended slowly in a winding route, so far as I could tell in the direction of the sea. Here and there we began to see the truth of Toby's guesses. Small scraped chambers cut out of the rock to each side were filled with crates of foreign origin. Finally the passage opened up into a larger chamber. Blackie lit all four lights around the sides of the room. No one was here before us. No Fluffs. We were alone with the dog.

He bared his teeth and growled loudly. I could feel my fur stand on end, as I backed up against the damp chalk wall. He laughed and stepped out, then barred the door behind him.

32

BETWEEN THE DEVIL AND THE DEEP BLUE SEA

Blackie had trapped us in the smugglers' cavern and I could see no way out. We might die a happy death there, for every other crate was full of French honeysuckle wine, or German nipjuice. But still I thought we would die. If we did not starve to death, the dog would surely come back and maul us. Or else Fluffs would come and take his revenge, secure from ever being found.

"Cheer up," said Toby, reading my thoughts.

"We're not dead yet. Have you seen what's in these crates? I think the first thing we should do is take a drink!"

So saying, he picked out a bottle, and pulled out the cork with a claw. I took a long draught of it too, and tried to calm my mind.

"There's a very great deal of stock here, don't you think?" said Toby.

"More, I should say, than the Black Horse alone could account for. Indeed, judging by the quality of this wine, I should think Mr Fluffs is supplying half of Brighton. But I wonder if he has been keeping all his eggs in one basket?"

Toby began to clamber on top of the crates, and soon reached the top of the teetering pile. He shouted down to me.

"It's here, by Great Bast's whiskers. We have him!" A few muffled oaths ensued, and a small chest fell down on top of me. I issued a few oaths of my own, and demanded to know what Toby was about.

He chuckled heartily. "Fluffs won't thank Blackie for locking us in here! Open it," he hissed, jumping down.

I could not. The chest was bound about with metal bands, and secured with a tight lock of an intricate kind.

"Have you your medical tools about you?"

"Well, no, I don't make it my habit to carry them everywhere!"

"A pity, I might have picked the lock." Toby took the chest from me and examined it closely. The wood was oak, it would not readily be broken apart. He set it down and pulled out one of the lamps from the wall. I had not noticed, but one of them had already gone out. We had only three left, and Bast knew how little time to make good our escape. I pointed this out.

"Ah very well" Toby sighed. "Shall we go then?"

"Certainly. How do you propose that we escape?" I could not help a little sarcasm. Toby is quite exasperating sometimes.

"By the other door, my dear fellow. It doesn't seem to be barred. Dogs are loyal, but this one is not the brightest."

"What door?"

"Oh, behind the crates, I noticed it just now."

We both clambered up the pile of crates, and there at the bottom of the pile behind them was another doorway, cut into the rock face. A rough wooden panel was wedged into it, but between us we wrenched it open without too much difficulty. The third lamp guttered out as we went through, and a blast of sea spray assaulted my nostrils. A short passage on through the chalk led to a small cave opening, its entrance obscured by small shrubs and ferns. We jumped down onto the beach at the base of the cliffs. For the moment then we were safe from Blackie, but still with no means of escape. A sheer cliff rose up above us, the sea advanced before us. A narrow strip of pebbles was our temporary home. I looked out to sea, and along the shore in both directions. There was no obvious means of assistance. Toby barely looked up. He was preoccupied with the chest.

"Brighton is that way," he declared, waving an airy paw. "But judging by the proximity of the sea, we should do better to head back to Rottingdean. It is just around the corner in that direction, and I noted a slipway down to the beach. Pass me that feather."

I took up the long feather he indicated, probably the wing feather of a seagull. He took it from me with a grunt, and stripped off the fluff, leaving a long quill. This he split carefully with his claw, flattening the end, and then addressed it to the lock. With a few subtle twists and turns it gave way, and the chest flew open. We did not spend that long examining the contents, and they will never be fully known, but believe me when I tell that it was a blackmailer's hoard the like of which could bring disaster on the nation. Fluffs' pursuit of power had known no bounds, respected no persons nor privacy. We had to destroy it. Toby secured the index to the contents which the meticulous Fluffs had included, and the rest I made ready to cast into the water. Toby stayed my paw.

"I think not, Robbie - too uncertain. We need fire for this. Happily Blackie was as careless with his possessions as he was with his prisoners."

Toby pulled out a tinderbox and scraped his claws along the side in a fast swipe. It lit at once, and he tipped the contents into the chest. It burned merrily to ashes. As it burned, I heard a loud anguished scream from the sea. I looked up. Corin Fluffs was approaching us in a small boat. It raced into the shore, and he sprang out, claws raised. Toby darted out of the way, and he fell onto the flaming chest. His scream of anguish turned into a scream of pain as the flames caught his fur. Unable to fight my instincts, I hurried forward and crushed the flames with my own body. Fluffs was broken. Burned by the fire, crushed by my own heavy frame, and bereft of his treasure, he lay on the beach amid the black seaweed and wept.

"No more to do here I think," said Toby. We left him there.

33

TO THE WINDMILL

We ran along the shore towards the slipway at Rottingdean, pebbles sliding under our paws, and the sea crashing closer with every breaking wave. A light drizzle was in the air, competing with the sea spray to douse our fur first in salt, then fresh water. When we stopped, breathless though I was, I had to demand some answers from Toby.

"Is there no more to be done with Fluffs? Was he not Richard's killer, even if he didn't kill Lucinda?"

"He has never been a killer - at least not by his own paws. That box full of poison might have led to a death, but it can do no more harm. Once his victims are notified that they are safe, I think his backers will melt away. The Grand Hotel will need a new manager soon enough. I rather think I might also write to our friend Shinycoat and see if he knows of someone suitable."

"But what will Fluffs do?"

"There is no curing a cat of that nature. We shall have to keep alert. But I think that this time he may have overreached himself. He had better take care."

"What do you mean?"

"When a blackmailer loses his power to threaten, he had better worry about who he has annoyed. You saw the names in that box. The great and the good of our society were among them; the four pillars of our establishment writ large. I should not care to have the weight of all four pillars determined to crush me. If Fluffs has not met with a nasty accident by the end of this week, I imagine he will have moved abroad."

"But can he not be jailed?"

"My dear fellow, how many times must I explain to you that there is nothing we can charge him with? I am sure that there is not one of his victims eager to appear in court. The judiciary especially not! No, he is broken enough, and I think he knows it. No doubt if we come across him again, it will be in a different line of employment."

"But what of the murders? Was he really nothing to do with it?"

"Certainly he was tangled in this business, and I think his habit of blackmail led many a cat to suppose that Lucinda meant to do the same. But she died for quite a different reason."

"Yes, her husband's jealousy. I still don't quite see who killed him though."

Toby shot me a curious look. He stared out to sea, the fur slicked against his body.

"We had better get dry, surgeon. Shall we go on to the Windmill?"

"Shouldn't we find Gertie and Vera first?"

"Oh they went straight there when we left them. Those were my instructions, anyway."

Despairing of any sense from this source, I wiped the dew from my whiskers and trotted behind Toby up the slope. The waves were now lapping hard against the cliffs, and I wondered if Fluffs had got back into his boat. We walked up and crossed the coastal path into the village. Fine old buildings of very ancient Yooman origin ranged on either side. A few had fallen down in the past, but the feline buildings and repairs had been kept of a piece so that one could almost imagine a Yooman face peering out from behind a curtain. We passed the Black Horse as quickly as we could and turned left up the hill towards the Red Windmill. Gertie and Vera stood at the door, with Miss Redclaw's maid Mittens between them, a pawkerchief dabbing at her nose.

"She's well then?" asked Toby.

Vera nodded. "And she knew it all along, the sly puss. Bells didn't know, though."

"Know what?" I demanded. Yet another secret was known by every person present before I had an inkling of it. Toby is the most frustrating of partners in detection.

"Whose daughter are you, Mittens?" said Vera, gently.

"I'm an orphan now," she sniffed. "Lucinda and Buttons were my parents, and now I am all alone in the world."

She began to wail loudly and Gertie clutched her close until she calmed, rubbing at her fur like a mother would a kitten. Toby is rarely moved by crying so much as inclement weather.

He motioned towards the skies and muttered, "Can't we question her in the dry at least?"

"Unfeeling brute," said Gertie, but she pulled Mittens inside the Mill, and we all followed.

"Their daughter?" I hissed under my breath, "But then how much more of a monster was Richard to kill the mother of his only kitten?"

"Certainly that would be the action of a fiend," said Toby. "However, it was not Richard who killed Lucinda. I am certain now that the same killer was responsible for both crimes."

"Who, why?" I spluttered.

"I can prove nothing yet, but I am hoping that this kit has some concrete point of proof for us."

Miss Redclaw had provided a room for us, and unexpectedly brought us all tea. She laid a kindly paw on the maid.

"There, there my child," she purred. "Drink that up while it's hot."

"You knew, I suppose?" said Toby.

"I knew of this kitten," she said, quietly.

"Yet you didn't think to mention her to myself or Gertie?"

"She ain't so strong as her mama," said Redclaw,

"And besides I had promised Lucinda to keep the secret. She's nothing to do with this devilment, I'm sure of it. You thought yourself it was Corin Fluffs."

"I was mistaken," said Toby, "Though I can tell you he is not likely to be any further trouble to you."

"We can buy our wine from our regular supplier again then? Blackie won't like it much. Not nearly so much profit in victualling cabbies." Toby lowered himself down to face Mittens, and gave her a gentle smile.

"I am sorry for your loss," he said, "and very glad to meet Lucinda's daughter. I have promised to catch your parents' killer. Will you help me?"

"If I can, sir" she whispered.

"Very well then, can you tell me anything about the night that Lucinda died?" She shook her head.

"I'm sorry I cannot. Papa and I were both here. We slept in our usual spots. Lucinda - Mama that is, meant to stay at the flat that night. She used to do it sometimes just to keep people off the trail."

I interrupted. "You mean it was a deliberate policy to hide the fact of your mother's married status?"

Mittens looked at me, bewildered. "Why yes, sir. There ain't many married actresses. They generally retire from the boards when they marry. But Ma and Pa had agreed that she should keep going. So we all kept it a secret, even from the rest of the performers here. They didn't talk to me much anyhow."

Toby gave me a meaning glance to hold my tongue, and bade her continue.

"I suppose you and your Papa visited her flat after she was found?"

"We did, just to look for her jewels, only they were all gone. She had a few letters and whatnot too, but I think the police had took them. We thought they must have taken the jewels too. We couldn't ask though, as Pa was afraid if they found out about us that they would think he had killed her."

"They might well have done so. What about the night that he died?"

Mittens sighed, and wiped away another tear with the back of her paw.

"Well, I was listening to the show from inside Pa's dressing room. I liked to hear him at work, and I wanted to be close to him, especially after Mama had died. When Victoria started wailing, I ran out, and I saw him dead. I didn't know what to do. I fainted. No one seemed to think much of it. But when I came round they had put me back in his dressing room. I thought it had just been a nightmare at first. Then I saw them on the dressing table."

"What?"

"These."

Mittens pulled a small silk bag out of her apron, and poured Lucinda's jewels out onto the floor. They sat there, flashing every colour of the rainbow at us, cold and hard and useless to an orphaned kitten. Vera gently took the bag from Mittens and swept them back up.

"Did you find anything else?" asked Toby.

"Anything out of place?"

Mittens thought, and shook her head. "No, not really. Only a bit of fluff on the floor, but that can't be what you mean."

"Was it this?" said Vera, and she held up a few brightly coloured threads, the very same as we had found clutched in Lucinda's claws.

34
SET A MAID

We left Mittens in the tender care of the surprising Miss Redclaw, who seemed to regard herself as some wise of Grandmama to the kit. I was convinced that Buttons had not been the killer. But then who was?

"We have eliminated a good many possibilities from our list, Robbie. What are we left with?"

"It was not Fluffs, not Mittens nor Redclaw. We are left with the 'Four Pillars' " I declared, gloomily.

"Quite right," said Toby, clapping me soundly on the shoulder.

"But it can't be any of them!" I growled crossly.

"And why not?"

I counted them off on my forepaw.

"Alleyfeather actually had an alibi for Buttons' killing. His train was here too late to have done the deed. The Prince had no need to kill her - she was not going to blackmail him."

"Leaving?"

"Judge Pennyclaw and Bishop Redfur. But I can't believe that either of them could have been the culprit."

"It is one of your most endearing features that you can never believe in the wickedness of your fellow cats until it is staring you in the face. I fear my nature is quite the reverse."

I gave Toby a rueful smile. He had been right many times in the face of my softer instincts.

"How can we trap the killer then? He has been very careful."

"Yes, that is so. But I think we may still have a trick or two at our disposal. We have some hard evidence at last. And a good many useful allies."

"Of course! The coloured threads - you know, when I saw them, I thought first of the Prince; his every costume includes some garish tie or sash."

"Royalty is often cursed by the need for sartorial volume. But the robes of every office can be brightly coloured."

"Of course! The Bishop's vestments. How disgusting that he would wear his robes of office in such an endeavour."

Toby was overtaken by a sudden fit of coughing but nodded at me through it. When he recovered himself he told me of his plan.

"We must confront our killer. These few threads will not be enough to hold him. We must break him down. I think a direct accusation will be enough."

"But we have already tried that!" I cried.

"We have interviewed each of these suspects ourselves, pressured them so much as can be done given their illustrious positions. Simply to say, 'You did it' won't work."

"Ah, but I plan to have the killer accused in front of some rather illustrious witnesses. And accused by another; by Lucinda's own daughter."

"She would do that?"

"I think she can be persuaded. But she will need a little coaching. This will be not so much a declaration as a short monologue."

"What?"

"She will need to say something that is not strictly true. But happily we have two excellent actresses on hand to assist her to learn her lines. And we shall see how much of her mother's talent she has inherited."

Three of our four pillars agreed to our plan, with varying degrees of reluctance. We gathered them the next morning at the train station under the clock. The Judge was first to arrive, strolling up from the street.

"I hope this will be over soon, Hunter. I shall need to be back to my chambers tomorrow."

"It will be over soon enough," said Toby, with an odd grin. Danny came next, appearing from amongst the crowds stepping off a London train.

"I suppose this is quite necessary? It is not long until the House reconvenes, and I may have to make a personal statement."

Toby merely blinked at him, and Danny fell silent.

The Bishop Redfur came last, arriving in a dog cart from Chichester. The hound was exhausted, and slunk away to get a drink. Redfur was in his regalia, and dusted himself down after jumping from the cart.

"Well?" he demanded. "There is surely nothing more to say."

"Perhaps nothing more for you to say, Bishop. But you will oblige me by listening to what this young kit has to add."

The Bishop turned to see Mittens stood beside him. She was in a state of some considerable agitation, breathing fast, eyes very wide. Gertie and Vera stood just behind her, in silent support.

"Who is this female?" he snapped rudely.

"I am the daughter of Lucinda Lexington and Richard Greywhiskers. I am maid at the Red Windmill. And I saw you do it! I saw you kill my father." She extended a trembling paw, claws out, pointing directly towards Danny Alleyfeather.

He gasped, unable for a moment to catch his breath.

"But you can't have done! There was no one else there." Then he realised what he had just said, and ran back towards the trains. We all froze, then first Toby and I ran after him. He leapt high over the barriers, and raced on towards the platforms. A locomotive was pulling in to the first platform, and behind it another was pulling out. Danny raced along, and leapt up in front of the first train, reaching out at full stretch towards the footplate of the departing carriage. He missed by a claw's length, and was struck by the incoming train, knocking him down onto the tracks. It rumbled on, pressing into the stoppers with a horrible crunch. Toby and I pulled up short, looking at each other in horror.

"That was not what I wanted. He should face justice! There should be a trial."

Judge Pennyclaw and the Bishop limped up behind us. The Bishop looked queasy, and pulled an amulet out of his robes.

"Ah, perhaps I should..." he began. But whatever cheering procedure the Bishop had intended to administer, it was never to be, as a low groan emitted from beneath the train.

"Excellent news, Toby," said the Judge "I rather think we can have a trial after all."

35
ENDINGS AND EXPLANATIONS

After an ambulance bristling with policecats had carted Danny away, the rest of us repaired to the waiting room, and equipped ourselves with a large brunch, including hot toasted muffins, grilled sardines, and cream tea. The Bishop declined, having had enough excitement to 'serve his life out' he hurried away to Chichester. The Judge poured the tea.

"Sugar, my dear?" he offered, patting Mittens' paw. "I don't suppose by any chance you really did see Alleyfeather do it? I shall have to recuse myself from the trial in any case, so you can tell me honestly."

"No, I didn't," she said, lowering her lashes. "But Mr Hunter said..."

"He is most persuasive, isn't he," said Pennyclaw. "Really, Hunter, sardine?" he passed one over "Really, I wish you would be less dramatic and deploy a bit of evidence rather than guesswork sometimes. It does add a great deal of difficulty to those of us in the legal profession."

"I think we had enough witnesses to his confession. And I'm sure a grieving daughter could be forgiven a small exaggeration."

"But how did she know who to accuse? You must have solved the case before."

"I told Mittens to point at the cat wearing the bright orange necktie." said Hunter, brushing some cream away from his whiskers.

"You probably noticed, Robbie, how he picked at it when he was nervous."

"Hmm" I applied myself to a muffin. "And that was your only clue?"

"Oh hardly. I was pretty sure of his guilt when he was the only cat with an apparent alibi for Greywhiskers' murder - that one was premeditated, after all."

"An apparent alibi."

"And sadly, of the simplest and most easily disproven nature. He lied about the time of his train. He actually arrived an hour before he told us, at two. He went straight to the Windmill and killed Greywhiskers. Then he went back to the hotel."

Vera said, "But why? A powerful, handsome cat like that. Why take such mad risks?"

"Love," said Hunter. "He told us the truth when he said that he had been in love with Lucinda, had wanted to marry her. It was a sort of madness. And when she laughed in his face, told him that she was already married, he did run mad. He killed her on the spot. But the second killing, that of Richard Greywhiskers, was a much more ugly matter. He finally realised the significance of Buttons who was always around. Perhaps he even went so far as to check at the records office. This, then was the husband who had stood in the way of his love. He decided to punish him."

"So that is why you feared for Mittens?"

"I didn't know if Danny knew of her existence or not. She could hardly be blamed for what had happened, but Alleyfeather was running mad. I wasn't sure what he would do."

I soothed Vera's paw, which trembled with anger or sorrow on the table. She gave me a grateful look. "Cats are strange," she said, "but most could not confuse love with greed."

"You are right," said Hunter, chastened. "I should not call that love. He wanted, I should say rather, to possess Lucinda, as his own. He could not bear to think that he had been bested in that." Suddenly, he leapt to his feet.

"Your Highness!"

"No need for formality, pray sit down," said Prince Hector, who had suddenly appeared in the waiting room, recalling us from low nosegreetings. "I got your invitation, Hunter, and you have been so very interesting, that I got up at your devilishly early suggested time and came to the station. I have been observing your antics from the gallery, and I conclude from the departure of the police that the business is finally done. Is it?"

"Your grace is very kind, and very correct," said Toby

"None of your sarcasm, thank you. But the Judge here is wrong. There will be no trial."

Toby began to protest, but Hector talked across him. "No, no, Hunter, it really will not do. Why only consider the witness list! Besides, my personal physician is taking a close interest in Alleyfeather on my behalf. He assures me that the cat will not live out the month. His injuries will certainly be fatal."

Toby bristled with anger. "Oh he assures you, does he?"

"If he has not yet, I don't doubt that he will assure me. I tend to be right about these things," said Hector. "Well, I must be off. You may attend the wedding, if you wish."

EPILOGUE

Final extract from the diary of Gertude Fluff

I am writing a postcard to Robbie. '*Glad you are not here*' is all I have managed so far. My companion has told me that this is an unacceptable sentiment, so I must think again. It is hard to think of anything much though when I am so happy. The Prince's wedding was a glorious affair. The Grand Duchess Tatiana and her maid did indeed grace it with their presence. The Prince seems to know his duty, and the nation is set fair to see the dynasty continue in its inexorable course. The newspapers were full of the Royal event, and very few paragraphs could be spared for the death of the Right Honourable Daniel Alleyfeather, MP, after a regrettable accident at a railway station. The wedding seemed to make Robbie even more mawkishly sentimental than usual. He could contain himself no longer, and proposed to Vera at the reception. She refused him, but he seemed to take it pretty well. I am rather glad, for I think the Doctor will remain ever susceptible to a pretty face. And she has brains enough to do rather more than interminably cater to his stomach. There was another strange incident there. Toby was most out of character, out of sorts for some reason, and accosted the Prince after the speeches. He insisted that some ancient bill was paid to a painter of Frescos, something to do with blue birds. The Prince was remarkably pleasant about it, but then he was no doubt braced for a difficult day, surrounded as he was by his own and his bride's relations. They were decked out with baubles, every cat, but Toby monopolised me to the extent that the Countess had no chance to pocket so much as a souvenir. I suppose I am done with my career as a jewel thief. I have found something better to do. For a long time we had heard no more from Corin Fluffs. Toby did spot some tale from China a month ago, which he seemed to think significant, but I persuaded him that it could likely be a trap as anything else, to get him out of the way and we did not go. But when the call came from Paris last week, Toby had to go. And he called on me. "Robbie won't leave just now he says his heart is broken. It's nonsense I know, but I have to go. And I need some help. Will you come with me?" It was not the most romantic of proposals, but I could never expect that from this cat. So we set off for France together. We were married this morning at the beautiful white chapel in Montmartre. I expect concealment, danger and mystery. I am so happy. Every day is a new adventure with Toby Hunter.

Milton Keynes UK
Ingram Content Group UK Ltd.
UKHW042135271124
451713UK00001B/5

9 781785 105531